The Last Vampire

Book Two

Other books by R. A. Steffan

The Horse Mistress: Book 1
The Horse Mistress: Book 2
The Horse Mistress: Book 3
The Horse Mistress: Book 4
The Complete Horse Mistress Collection

The Lion Mistress: Book 1
The Lion Mistress: Book 2
The Lion Mistress: Book 3
The Complete Lion Mistress Collection

The Dragon Mistress: Book 1
The Dragon Mistress: Book 2

Antidote: Love and War, Book 1
Antigen: Love and War, Book 2
Antibody: Love and War, Book 3

The Queen's Musketeers: Book 1
The Queen's Musketeers: Book 2
The Queen's Musketeers: Book 3
The D'Artagnan Collection: Books 1-3
The Queen's Musketeers: Book 4

Sherlock Holmes & The Case of the Magnate's Son

Diamond Bar Apha Ranch
Diamond Bar Alpha 2: Angel & Vic
(with Jaelynn Woolf)

The Last Vampire

Book Two

R. A. Steffan & Jaelynn Woolf

The Last Vampire: Book Two

For information, contact the author at
http://www.rasteffan.com/contact/

Cover art by Deranged Doctor Design

First Edition: December 2018

Author's Note

This book contains graphic violence and explicit sexual content. It is intended for a mature audience.

Table of Contents

One

"Whoa. I feel, really drunk all of the sudden." I stared at the blank concrete walls of the cell I was sharing with my unsmiling Fae captor. My unfocused eyes moved to the half-empty cup I was holding, and then to Albigard himself, regarding me from across the room. I blinked rapidly, trying to clear my blurry double vision. "Why do I feel drunk all of the sudden?"

Rans had sent me back to the creepy basement dungeon with Albigard when it became clear there weren't any useful clues to my father's disappearance to be found in his ransacked condo. After less than an hour in Albigard's company, I was already wishing that I'd kicked up more of a fuss about returning here with him alone.

"You are drunk because you can't hold your drink, presumably," the Fae suggested, raising an eyebrow at me.

Albigard waved a graceful hand, and the cup disappeared from my grip, leaving my fingers grasping nothing. I stared at them stupidly for a moment.

"What was in that stuff, anyway?" I asked, readjusting my feet until the ground stopped tilting to the left. For some reason, it was becoming hard to get the words to come out right unless I spoke very slowly and clearly. My eyes narrowed. "Rans is gonna be pished… I mean, *pissed*… if you slipped me a faerie roofie when he wasn't looking." I cocked my head, thinking about that for a moment before adding, "And I'm gonna be pished, too."

"It was *mead*," my not-really-a-captor said, "and you're already pissed, it appears. I gave it to you because you said you were thirsty. Perhaps you could return your focus to what we were discussing before?"

I pondered that for a few seconds, frowning. Perhaps I could… if I could *remember* what we'd been discussing before. I tried to shake some brain cells loose after what had legitimately been a day from hell. We'd been at my dad's place, looking through the destruction for any hint as to what had happened to him or where he'd been taken. There weren't any obvious clues to speak of, which didn't seem to surprise either Rans or Albigard.

One thing I was quickly coming to understand about supernatural creatures was that they were a bunch of arrogant, high-handed assholes. The Fae had insisted we leave before our presence drew unwanted attention from anyone else who might be watching the apartment. Rans said something about talking to some people he knew who might be able to help.

"Take her back to the house," he'd told Albigard. "I'll join you there shortly."

At which point his body had swirled away into a cloud of vapor, leaving me on my own with a hotter—and much more disturbing—version of Legolas from *Lord of the Rings*. The Fae had opened the same kind of magical portal he'd used to transport us to my father's home in the first place, and when I'd stepped through, I was back in the basement cell we'd left earlier.

Alone.

With a member of a species that apparently wanted me dead.

"I'm not having sex with that vampire bastard again until he apologizes for this," I stated, scowling.

Albigard stared at me with flat green eyes. "This is the sort of information that I'd really prefer not to have," he said, "if it's all the same to you."

I stared back, confused, since I hadn't been talking to him. "Huh?" I asked, only to cut him off as another thought surfaced from the murky depths. "Oh! Right, I remember now. You were saying about the demons…?"

That was kind of important, wasn't it? I should try not to forget about it again. Albigard had remained here in the basement under the guise that he was still interrogating Rans and me. I'd been asking him about the treaty between his people and the demons. That was right before I mentioned I was thirsty, and he'd conjured the magical cup of roofie-mead out of thin air for me to drink.

More fool him. Didn't he know that if he tried to take advantage of me, I could pull his life force out through his dick?

Succubus, baby. Suck it!

I laughed, surprised when it emerged as a stupid sounding, high-pitched giggle. Oh, yeah…

drunk. I'd forgotten about that part for a second as well.

"Wow, this really blows," I said, as the walls started moving again. After a moment, I steadied my shoulder against the nearest one so I wouldn't accidentally fall over if the floor decided to get in on the action.

Albigard's expression said he didn't intend to argue with my assessment.

"If you've quite regained control of yourself," he began in that snooty Fae tone that I was growing to hate, "then I'll continue."

It was the kind of tone that said anyone who wasn't Fae must clearly be an idiot. But I could choose to be the bigger person here. I waved a careless hand. "Whatever. Do go on."

He sighed, long-suffering. "I was saying that the reason you and your father have become such sought-after targets is two-fold. You already know about the treaty provision forbidding demonic interference in the human realm."

"Uh-huh." I nodded sagely, trying to keep my *serious business* face in place. Nigellus had told me about that part when we were in Atlantic City, after all.

"There is a larger concern among the Fae, however," Albigard continued. "The entire point of the treaty is to limit demonkind's ability to grow in strength. They must not be allowed to gain so much power that they once again threaten us."

But that was stupid.

"Look, Tinkerbell," I said, jabbing a finger at him. "My dad's just a normal guy, right? He's a fucking accountant, for god's sake. And look at me!" I gestured up and down the length of my body, gaining steam. "I'm a waitress! Not even that—I'm an *ex-waitress*! Because you and your creepy blond faerie friends *lost me my job!*"

My righteous anger seemed to be entirely wasted on my current audience. Which kind of sucked, to be honest. I settled for frowning at him severely, since if I tried to go over and kick him in the kneecap, I was afraid I might fall down. Or, y'know, die a horrible, agonizing death at the hands of faerie magic.

One or the other.

Albigard sighed again. He seemed to be doing that a lot. "You're a second-generation succubus-human hybrid. You are aware that until now, demons have never been able to sustainably reproduce?"

I picked my way through the words, most of which seemed to have too many syllables. "Kind of?" The brief conversation with Nigellus ran through my head again. "I know they can't die, and that subbucusses… *succubuses*…"

"Succubi," Albigard offered, long-suffering.

"Succ-u-bi," I echoed carefully, "have to hijack humans to make babies."

"Offspring which should be completely sterile," Albigard continued, "not that such behavior is permitted anymore, since the treaty came into force."

"Didn't stop my grandad, did it?" I muttered.

"Clearly not." The Fae sounded like he'd tasted something sour. "If the demons discover that they can... *breed*... generationally, they may decide to make a grab for power, and damn the treaty provisions. It would mean war again."

He'd looked positively green when he was talking about demons breeding, but at the mention of war, something about his face changed. If I wasn't so busy trying to keep my knees locked so I stayed upright, I might've wondered at it.

"This whole thing is really, really stupid," I decided.

His expression changed again. *That* one was easier to decipher. It was anger.

"You're talking about my race's survival," Albigard ground out, something dangerous and alien peeking out from behind the paper-thin facade of that pretty-boy face.

I tried to push away from the wall, only to decide that standing unaided was overrated. Instead, I settled on jabbing a pointed finger toward him again. "Yeah?" I asked combatively. "Well, your buddies don't sheem all that worried about *my* shurvival, now do they?"

Was I slurring again? Damn it...

"You are one person," Albigard said in an icy tone. "There are countless thousands of Fae lives in the balance—"

A vaporous mist swirled through the high basement window above us. I watched in fascination as it materialized into the solid form of Rans, the process more riveting than the coolest CGI imaginable. His blue gaze flicked between us.

"And we all know how quick the Fae are to sacrifice individuals to the greater good," Rans said, his gaze settling heavily on Albigard.

The Fae's expression grew stony, but I ignored it.

"Hi!" I said cheerfully, shoving away from the wall and catching myself against Rans' chest instead.

One of his arms circled my shoulders to steady me as he looked down at me in surprise. I smiled up at him, ridiculously happy that he'd come back. A moment later, I remembered that I was supposed to be angry with him for leaving in the first place,

"You left me alone with a faerie," I accused, aiming for a glower and ending up with something that felt more like a pout. "You suck."

Maybe it would have had more impact if I weren't hanging all over him.

His brows drew together. "Are you *drunk*?"

I started to giggle, only to have it end on a hiccup. "Tinkerbell roofied me," I said. "With *mead.* I told him you'd be pissed about it."

"I think you're the one who's pissed," he said, though his eyes did start to glow with that unearthly inner light.

"Off her arse," Albigard agreed.

That gas-flame glow turned on him. "You tricked her into accepting a Fae gift. Why?"

Oooh… I'd been right. Rans was *not pleased.* I turned my attention to Albigard. It felt kind of like watching a tennis match.

"Because that is how the game is played, as you well know," the Fae said, apparently unconcerned.

My eyes tracked back to Rans.

"You're quickly burning through whatever goodwill I had stored up, Albigard."

"Whereas you are making me question whether your association is useful enough to be worth the hassle, bloodsucker."

Now I was starting to get dizzy again. I tugged on Rans' sleeve. "Hey. Someone wanna explain using short words?"

Rans looked down at me again, his face still set in hard planes. "You accepted Fae drink."

Well… yeah? Hadn't we covered that part already?

"It was, like, half a cup!" I protested. "And it wasn't even all that good!"

"Not the point," Rans said tightly. "Accepting gifts from the Fae gives them power over you."

"Oh." I blinked. "Okay, that seriously blows. You'd think someone might've, I dunno, warned me about that *before he left me alone with one for an hour*?"

A muscle ticked in the corner of Rans' jaw. I stared at it, fighting the sudden urge to lick along its tempting length.

"*Someone* thought he could trust the sparkly little arsehole to behave for an hour," he said, and Albigard bristled. "Besides, doesn't your generation read fairy tales anymore? I mean, is it seriously *not* common knowledge that you don't eat Fae food or drink Fae wine?"

"It wasn't wine!" I pointed out.

Albigard's unruffled act seemed to really be slipping now. He stepped up until he was practically in Rans' face, glaring at him from a slight advantage of height.

"And *do* you trust me, bloodsucker?" he asked.

"About as far as I can throw you, Fae," Rans replied, his voice level.

"Oh?" Albigard tilted his head. "How far do you think that is?"

Rans grinned, fangs peeking out. "Let's hope we don't have to find out."

I poked him in the chest. "Could we maybe compare dick sizes some other time?" I asked, and then frowned, meeting Albigard's eyes. "I mean... don't get me wrong, though. His is pretty big." I hooked a thumb at Rans.

The Fae gave me the same vaguely nauseated look he'd given me when we'd been talking about demons breeding with humans. "I believe we already discussed my lack of interest in your sex life."

"Your loss," I muttered. "My sex life is *brilliant* now."

Rans tried and failed to stifle a quiet, choked noise. Then he changed the subject.

"I've found some people who may be able to provide us with more information," he said, turning his attention back to Albigard with a bit less threat in his manner. "Which means you'll be cutting us loose now, in case that's not already clear."

The Fae lifted a sharp eyebrow. "Does it? And will you be sharing the results of your inquiries with me if I '*cut you loose*'?"

"Yes," Rans said. "When *don't* I, Tinkerbell?"

"Whoa there, cowboy," I interrupted. "Is it really a good idea to share stuff with..." I gestured vaguely. "... one of them?"

"He trusts me as far as he thinks he can throw me," Albigard said in a voice as dry as the desert.

"And I expect I could throw him pretty far, if I had to," Rans agreed. "It's not his fault he's an irritating wanker most of the time."

There were important undercurrents here... probably. But I was drunk, so—

"Okay, whatever. Can we leave now?"

Albigard looked like he'd be happy to see the back of me. That was fine. I'd be happy to see the back of him, too—and not just because he had a nice ass. I wasn't interested in his ass. Not when the rest of him made me feel so creepy crawly. Besides, I had a better ass right here. My hand crept down to squeeze it, and Rans shot me an, '*Oh my god, seriously?*' look that I ignored completely.

"I'll glamour you again and return you to the airport," Albigard said, his eyes trailing down to my offending hand on Rans' ass.

He was probably jealous, and he should be. I grinned at him, wide and stupid, the expression growing even wider and stupider when I saw the pinched look on his stupid Fae face. Hey—if he didn't want me drunk, he shouldn't have roofied me with faerie mead, right?

Magic flowed over us, and the muscular globe I was grasping grew a bit softer and squishier. I looked down to see that I was once more pale and curvy rather than slim and dusky. I looked up, and sure enough, Rans was now ash blonde and plain-faced.

"I'll summon the guards and let them know that you weren't of use to me," Albigard said. "When they arrive, act disoriented."

"Shouldn't be a problem," Rans said, the words dripping with irony. "Not for one of us, at least."

"No. I daresay it won't," agreed the Fae, giving me a final, disdainful look.

Albigard dropped us off with our luggage along the same stretch of the arrivals and departures lane where he'd scooped us up. On some level, I was starting to wonder why I didn't seem to be getting any more sober as time passed. Maybe I should also be wondering why I was drunk on half a cup of alcohol in the first place, but somehow that seemed like an awful lot of stuff to try to keep track of at the same time.

"So," I asked once the black Mercedes had disappeared into traffic, "who're these people we need to talk to?"

Rans eyed me up and down with his boring, not-blue gaze before replying. "Let's worry about them after we worry about getting you rested and sobered up."

I pouted a little, before realizing that getting me rested and sobered up would presumably involve a bed. "Yes! Beds are brilliant!" I told him. "I love beds."

"O-*kay*, then," he said, still watching me like he wasn't quite sure what I'd do or say next. I could sympathize with that. I wasn't quite sure either.

I grinned and let him flag down a taxi, which he paid for with cash. For some reason, I'd sort of assumed we'd be going to a hotel. Instead, the cab wended its way through airport traffic until we got on a highway, heading into an area that looked residential. Eventually, we ended up in a nice suburban neighborhood, and the taxi driver dropped us off in front of an attractively landscaped split-level home.

"Another friend of yours?" I asked, wondering just how many people Rans actually knew in Chicago.

He snorted. "Not hardly. I have no idea who lives here—in fact, I chose the address at random from Google Maps. Come on. Follow my lead."

I shrugged and followed him to the door. He rang the doorbell, which was answered within moments by a pleasant-looking middle-aged woman. She eyed our suitcases with thinly veiled curiosity, a small furrow appearing between her neatly plucked eyebrows.

"May I help you?" she asked.

Beside me, Rans' gaze burned with inner light through the muddy brown of the Fae glamour. "Invite us in."

She gave us a vague smile. "Come in, please."

We stepped into the foyer. The door closed behind us.

"Tell me who lives here with you." Rans' voice was compelling.

"Just my husband Tom," she replied, still smiling. "He's downstairs."

"Very good," said Rans. "Are there any pressing reasons why you and he couldn't leave for the weekend?"

She appeared to give it a moment's consideration. "No."

"Call him up here for me."

"Tom!" the woman yelled. "Come here for a minute!"

I winced a bit at the volume. Footsteps pounded up the stairs, and a florid-faced man appeared.

"What's going on, Glynda?" he demanded, giving us a suspicious look before Rans' eyes caught and held him.

"Hullo, Tom," Rans said. "Do you concur with your wife that this would be a good time for a weekend getaway?"

Tom's eyes lit up with interest. "Yes. This would be a good time for a weekend getaway, Glynda. We should go to the lake house."

Glynda nodded. "What a good idea! Let's go to the lake house."

"Got enough money to cover the trip?" Rans asked, addressing both of them.

"Oh, yes," Glynda said. "Our investments did especially well last quarter."

"I'm pleased to hear it," Rans told her. "We're your house sitters. You're going to pack and leave in the next thirty minutes, so we'll just wait here while you do."

"Thank you for agreeing to house sit for us on such short notice," Glynda enthused. "It really means a lot to us."

Rans smiled as Tom put an arm around his wife's shoulders and squeezed, nodding in dazed agreement.

"It's our pleasure," Rans assured them. "Oh, and you'll want to leave us the keys to the second car when you go."

"Of course!" Glynda chirped. "It's in the garage. I just filled up the tank last Tuesday."

With that, the couple bustled off, presumably to pack. Rans and I showed ourselves to the upstairs living room to wait. I stared at the ugly print pattern of the sofa and chairs, which seemed to waver back and forth in a disturbing moiré pattern before my drunken eyes.

I must've zoned out for a bit, because it seemed like less than half an hour had passed when Glynda called a cheery goodbye, the door opening and closing as she and her husband left, suitcases in hand. I narrowed my eyes at Rans, who lounged carelessly in the far corner of the sofa, one ankle propped on the opposite knee.

"That," I said slowly, "was creepy as hell."

Two

Rans shrugged one shoulder, unconcerned. "Being creepy is in the vampire contract, somewhere below the part about good dental hygiene and needing SPF ten million before spending a day at the beach."

I digested that for a few moments.

"Why am I still drunk?" I asked. "In fact, why am I drunk at all? Did Tinkerbell really roofie me? Because if so, I feel like you should have beat him up for me before we left."

His air of casual relaxation faded, his expression growing serious. "Half a cup of Fae mead shouldn't have made you drunk, no. But I think you roofied yourself, luv."

I glared at him, offended. "Did *not*!"

But he only shook his head. "You attacked Alby by drawing on his animus. *Fae* animus. I imagine all the Fae magic you swallowed when you did that interacted with the Fae magic in the drink. Your demon blood probably made the effect even worse." A brief smile tugged up one corner of his lips. "Face it, Zorah—you're well and truly sloshed on faerie juice."

I couldn't help it—I started snickering. Rans rose gracefully from the couch and pulled me to my feet, slinging an arm around me so he could guide me into the kitchen. Once there, he poured me into a chair at the breakfast nook… thingie, and started puttering around in the refrigerator.

I slumped forward, resting my forehead on my arms—still smiling, though I couldn't have said why. On some level, I knew there was a whole lot of stuff going on that wasn't remotely smile-worthy, but it all seemed oddly distant and unimportant right now.

Maybe I dozed a little, because when the sound of a plate landing on the table in front of me jerked me upright, there was drool on my left forearm. A large glass of water and a couple of little white aspirin joined the plate, which appeared to have a sandwich on it. My mouth watered. I grabbed for the food and took a big bite without even thinking, my eyes slipping closed in ecstasy at the taste. An almost sexual groan slipped past my lips.

"You're welcome," Rans said in a wry tone, seating himself in the other chair. "I do *so* appreciate a woman with a healthy appetite."

Something important occurred to me at the same instant I swallowed, almost making me choke. Coughing a bit, I reached for the water glass.

"Shit," I managed when my throat was clear. "Wait. Sorry. I can't eat this. I'm gluten-intolerant."

Rans raised a glamoured blonde eyebrow at me. "You're not gluten-intolerant. You're a succubus-human hybrid who was starved of sex for… how long? I'm impressed that you were able to manage your malnutrition with lifestyle alterations for as long as you did, but trust me when I say—on the list of things that are likely to kill you right now, sandwich bread is quite near the bottom."

I stared at him, and then I stared at the sandwich in my hands.

"Do vampires have really good hearing?" I asked.

"Yes," Rans replied slowly, obviously unsure where I was going with that.

I nodded. "Good. In that case, your punishment if you're lying to me will be to stand outside the bathroom door during my hour-long bout of explosive diarrhea."

He sighed. "I'm not lying to you."

I shrugged and devoured the sandwich.

At his prompting, I also drank the water and swallowed the aspirin. Then I let him lead me to what I gathered was the guest bathroom, where he rummaged around until he found an unopened toothbrush in a cabinet drawer. I brushed my teeth, eyed the shower stall warily, and decided in a shining moment of self-preservation that I was quite likely to fall down and split my head open in my current state. Maybe that was what Rans had meant about gluten being low on the list of things that would kill me?

I stumbled out of the bathroom and into the bedroom across from it, to find that Rans was waiting there, standing near the bed. He'd shed his glamour. That was good. I was one seriously shallow bitch when I was drunk, apparently, and Mr. Blonde and Forgettable just wasn't on the same shag-ability scale as his real appearance.

"Hi," I said, a bit breathlessly. Without really intending it, I'd plastered myself against his body. I breathed in deeply, taking in his scent.

I felt his small huff of amusement more than I heard it. He let me pull him down to press our mouths together for only a moment before he pulled back, capturing my wrists in a gentle grip and easing me away.

I frowned. "What's wrong?"

He kissed the furrow in my brow. "You're the one who keeps saying you've been roofied, luv. You need sleep right now more than you need a top-up. Get all that Fae shite out of your system first, and hit on me again later if your hangover isn't too atrocious."

A sinking sensation pulled at my stomach. For the first time since drinking the mead, all of the circling thoughts and fears surrounding the past few days threatened to descend and crush me beneath their weight once more. I caught at Rans' arm, distantly aware of how pathetic I was about to look.

"Stay anyway," I breathed.

He stilled, and I realized that it was the first time I'd asked him for something bigger and more important than sex. Damn it, damn it, *damn it.* Being drunk was the absolute *worst.* Mentally berating myself, I drew breath to backtrack before he could point out how ridiculous I was being.

I was too slow.

"You should be careful, Zorah," he said. "I'm not a good person to trust in that way."

I held his gaze for a long moment. "Then stop rescuing me, goddamn it," I shot back, anger swelling to join my humiliation.

And that was reasonable, wasn't it? If you didn't want a girl to start trusting you, then you shouldn't save her from monsters. You shouldn't protect her and watch over her and say nice things to her, if you were just going to pull away and pretend later on that you were no good for her.

Huh. Apparently I'd stymied him, at least temporarily. Twice, he started to speak before stopping himself. Finally, he settled on, "Lie down on the bed, Zorah. I'll stay with you until you fall asleep."

My stomach unknotted itself, and I nodded. Crap, it was pretty clear I'd slid past the fun part of being drunk and into the depressed, weepy part. That was bad. I needed to keep my damned mouth shut before I started sounding like even more of a pathetic, whiny bitch than I already was.

I could do that. Sure I could. I mean, how hard could it be?

I sat on the bed and kicked off my boots. Deciding that the rest of my clothing wasn't worth the effort of dealing with, I rolled onto my side, turning my back to the room. After a moment's hesitation, the mattress dipped and a cool body slotted in behind me. Another pregnant pause, and an arm wrapped around my waist.

An ache built in my throat. I'd had so little of this in my life. Could I trust it, when I'd practically had to beg for it before he agreed to give it to me?

Eventually, Rans broke the pensive silence. "You're terrible at guarding your heart, aren't you," he said, not really phrasing it as a question. "You told me your father was a passive-aggressive arsehole, and yet you were ready to charge in and save him without a plan... or even a single bit of backup." He paused for a beat before adding, "I admire you for that... even if it scares me half to death."

The ache grew worse. "I *have to,* though." The words slipped past my self-imposed wall of silence. "I have to know if— "

I cut myself off sharply.

"You have to know whether he intended to help you or betray you," Rans finished for me.

I thought of all the hurtful words my father had hurled at me over the years. All of the distance. The neglect. The emotional abuse.

You're going to come to a bad end, Zorah—just like your mother.

I never wanted a child like you, Zorah. Why did you have to be like this?

On the cusp of adulthood, I often found myself wondering why no one had intervened on my behalf as a child. Where was everyone else in the family? Where were my teachers and school counselors? But the answer was pretty obvious. My family members were dead, distant, or mentally unwell. My teachers were overworked, a bit freaked out by my strangeness, and quite possibly taken in by my long-perfected act of everything being okay.

And it hurt. It hurt that no one had cared enough to see the truth of things. It hurt that no one had thought to check in on a grieving widower with a six-year-old daughter, and make sure they were coping all right.

Because we hadn't been coping. Not even close.

How much of that was the fault of a man who'd just seen his wife shot to death in front of his eyes? A man who—if I was to believe what I'd learned in the past few days—might well have been damaged in unseen ways by the years spent with my mother?

I had no idea.

"He's all I have left," I choked, and… *shit*. My cheeks were wet. I was drunk-crying now, complete with tears and snot and puffy eyes and clogged sinuses.

"I know," Rans said softly, the arm around me tightening.

That arm didn't let go until much later, after I'd drunk-cried my stupid, drunk ass to sleep.

Hours later, the pounding throb of my headache woke me. I wasn't sure exactly how much time had passed, but it was dark outside the bedroom window. I'd expected to be alone, abandoned to my pathos the instant Rans thought he could get away from me without triggering more waterworks.

Instead, I was wrapped around him, drooling on his shirt, the ever-expanding circle of dampness cool against my cheek. My eyes felt like sandpaper. When I raised my aching head, my hair tugged against my scalp where his fingers had become tangled in the matted spirals.

"How do you feel?" he asked, and even his low voice was enough to drive a spike through my left temple.

"Like I've been roofied on faerie juice and then made a complete fool of myself," I mumbled, the sound of my reply driving in a few more spikes for good measure. "*Ow.*"

Those long fingers kneaded my nape. "Shower. More water. More aspirin," he said, focusing on the practical. "Then come back to bed. It's the middle of the night. There's nothing that needs doing until morning."

I bit my lip and nodded, afraid that if I made any further mention of my drunken breakdown, it would give the whole thing more power, somehow. As it was, I could pretend it had all… I don't know. Been a dream or something.

"Okay. Uh… sorry about your shirt." I rolled upright, gesturing vaguely at the drool-stain.

"I've survived worse, believe me," he said.

An image of bloodstains and cratered flesh flashed in front of my eyes, making me shiver.

"Yeah," I said. "I know you have."

I gingerly eased off of the bed, glad beyond measure that Glynda and Tom had demonstrated the thoughtfulness to put a nightlight in the guest bathroom. That saved me from having to turn on an overhead light, which I suspect would have been excruciating.

The bathroom was well stocked, but I dragged my overnight bag in with me anyway so I could rummage for my hair-pick and conditioner. The mirror revealed what I hadn't quite realized before—Albigard's glamour had worn off while I slept. I stared at my reflection as though seeing it for the first time. Red, puffy eyes stared back at me.

The cup by the sink looked clean, so I filled it with cool water and followed Rans' advice with the painkillers. I showered in the near-dark, letting the hot water and steam clear out my head as much as anything could right now.

There was something to be said for being clean and moisturized, even under circumstances as sucktastic as these. I decided that my best strategy for now was definitely going to be denial.

Drunken breakdown? What drunken breakdown?

I have no memory of this drunken breakdown of which you speak.

Rans was born in the Middle Ages. People were big on chivalry back then. I felt reasonably confident he wouldn't rub my nose in it if I decided to play dumb about the whole thing. I slipped on my black silk nightie and headed back to the bedroom on tiptoe, praying that Rans had fallen asleep in my absence.

Rans... had not fallen asleep in my absence.

Instead, Rans was lying naked on the bed, his upper body resting against a pile of pillows. I actually felt his sexual energy flowing across the room to me before I registered his hand sliding slowly up and down his cock in the faint light of the moon streaming through the window.

My heart fluttered before settling into a strong, steady rhythm, my blood humming beneath my skin. The dull throbbing behind my eyes eased, as though someone had placed a cool cloth over my forehead.

Dear god above, this man was beautiful when he was naked. Hell, he was beautiful when he *wasn't* naked, but that didn't mean I was going to squander this opportunity to stare at all those sleek muscles layered under skin that glowed silver in the moonlight. I hardly registered the slow sigh that escaped me, taking the rigid tension in my shoulders with it.

"Thought this might help a bit more than aspirin," he said, his free hand cradling the back of his head as he leaned against the headboard.

"Uh-huh," I breathed, watching the play of his chest muscles as more of that replenishing power flowed into me. *Jesus.* Every time I got to experience this, I felt like I should be pinching myself because it couldn't possibly be real. It couldn't possibly be this... *good.* With difficulty, I tore my attention away from all that pale skin to ask, "Are you sure about this?"

I broke off, silently berating myself. *Idiot.* Did I really want to remind him that he was offering to sex up an emotional wreck with daddy issues? *Of course I didn't.*

Quickly changing tack, I said, "I mean, do you want some of my blood first? So I don't wipe you out as badly?"

His lips pursed in distaste, the brief expression followed by a wry, lopsided smile. "If it's all the same to you, I'll wait until the rest of Tinkerbell's animus makes its way out of you. Fae life force isn't really to my taste."

I was still glued in place in the doorway. Part of me was screaming, *'Are you mentally deficient, girl? Why are you standing all the way over here when you could be on the bed?'* But the rest was fixated on a new question.

"Why do I react so strongly to you?" I asked. "And not just you. Albigard, too—although his energy made me feel like insects were crawling under my skin. I'd never felt like this with anyone I slept with before I met you. I had no idea I was drawing *anything* from them... but with you, I can feel it happening. Hell, if I close my eyes, I can practically *see* it."

Rans released himself, lacing his fingers behind his head as he considered his reply. Immediately, I felt the flow of energy slow to a trickle.

"They were all human," he said. "Fae and vampire animus is stronger. Demon, too, I imagine. Our life force is bolstered by magic. It's not surprising that as demonkin, Fae magic doesn't agree with you. The two races have been enemies for longer than humans have been walking upright on two legs."

"Guess I'm lucky that vampire animus is demon-compatible, in that case," I said lightly.

"You know what they say," he replied in the same tone. "Once you go undead, you never go back."

I chuckled. "That's a terrible slogan. You need a better copywriter."

He shrugged. "The pay's shite and the hours are worse. Makes it hard to find good talent." A dark eyebrow cocked. "Now get your arse over here, unless you just want to stand there and play voyeur all night."

Honestly, I could think of worse things than watching Rans unselfconsciously fisting that gorgeous cock—but even *that* would be better when viewed close up.

"Maybe I've just discovered a secret voyeurism kink," I told him as I crossed to the foot of the bed. "Is that a succubus thing?"

He snorted. "All kinks are a succubus thing, luv. It sort of comes with the territory." His head tilted in interest. "So, do you have any others?"

Three

Okay, that was a rather unexpected question—though maybe it shouldn't have been. Was this what sex partners normally did, when they weren't too busy running for the hills after sleeping with you? Asking about your likes and dislikes, feeling out your kinks?

Shit, maybe it was.

Too bad my only experience of healthy relationships came from reading trashy romance novels where the hero magically knew the heroine's every secret desire. And sure, some of those sexy scenes did more for me than others, but there was a big difference between reading about something and wanting to do it… or wanting to have it done to you.

"I have absolutely no idea about my kinks," I said eventually, deciding honesty was the best policy in this situation. "Mostly, I'm into guys not treating me like a nympho freak for wanting to get laid." *And for wanting to nibble on their life force like it was a Sunday buffet,* I didn't add.

Rans didn't move from his relaxed sprawl, though a smile twitched at his lips. "Then you appear to be in luck, Zorah Bright… though I still think we can do better than that. Look around you… nice big house, all to ourselves. Solid construction. Far enough away from the neighbors that no one will hear you screaming your head off when I make you come for the dozenth time."

And just like that, the flesh between my thighs was aching and throbbing, demanding satisfaction. Judging by his smug expression, the vampire on the bed knew it, too. *Bastard.*

"Your modesty is one of your most attractive qualities, you know. So, what about you?" I asked, trying to turn it back on him. "What does a vampire do for kicks in bed?"

His expression turned jaded for a moment before he consciously smoothed it. "After seven hundred years, just about everything you can imagine, at one time or another. And probably a few things you can't."

I remembered the afternoon at Nigellus' house in Atlantic City—how Rans had urged me to use him until exhaustion finally quieted his circling thoughts.

"You use sex to make everything stop for a bit, don't you?" I said in a burst of insight. "That's why you don't seem to care that I'm draining you when you sleep with me. Being drained helps you turn it all off for a while."

Still, he didn't move—and yet I thought I could sense walls coming up.

"It's cheaper than therapy," he said, throwing a quip I'd made to Guthrie back at me. The smile he flashed was tight, and didn't reach his eyes. "Besides, it gets terribly tiresome having to wipe a therapist's memories after every single session. Hard to make any progress that way."

"I bet."

Was it strange that I felt better knowing we were both kind of fucked up in the head? Maybe it was because I could pretend we were on equal ground that way. It made me feel less like the stereotypical pathetic girl relying on the competent, kick-ass man—or rather, the competent, kick-ass *vampire*. Instead, I could tell myself we were two messed-up people coming together, and that I had something to offer him, too. Even if that 'something' was nothing more than an hour or two of sexually mediated oblivion.

"You haven't really answered the question, though," I prodded, finally breaking free of my paralysis. I crossed to the bed and sank down on the edge, half facing him. Because I could, I placed a hand over his silent heart—where a shotgun blast had torn through the smooth flesh mere days ago—holding it there for a moment before running it down the hard ridges of his stomach. "What do *you* like?"

It was like caressing a statue... or it would have been if his cock hadn't twitched against his belly. Blue eyes held mine.

"Oh, I could fill a century or three with all the things I want to do to you, my little vixen," he said. "But honestly, I've found that *what* you do in bed is far less important than *who* you're doing it with."

My breath caught. *Not fair, damn it.* He shouldn't be allowed to make my heart and my sex ache at the same time. That was playing dirty.

"Don't say things like that," I whispered, my hand still splayed low on his abdomen.

There was a moment's silence. "You really don't do well with kindness, do you, Zorah?" he observed. Then he raised a challenging eyebrow. "Fair enough. If you don't want to hear it, then come here and shut me up."

That sounded like a plan I could get behind. I leaned forward, closing the distance until I could kiss him at the same time I slid my hand down the final few inches to encircle his erection. My eyes slid closed as the sensation of something flowing out of him and into me returned. He let me ravish his mouth and cock for a few minutes, drawing what I needed from him.

Then his hands closed on my shoulders and his body twisted under me. Before I was aware of what was happening, I was on my back beneath him, caged by his hard body as his weight pressed me into the soft mattress. His mouth grew demanding on mine, and something inside me loosened, settling warmly into place.

Eventually, the feeling of drowning in him grew too intense, forcing me to wrench my lips free of his so I could gasp in air. "This," I panted. "I want this. I want you to make me lose control."

If I could help him turn everything off for a while, maybe he could do the same for me. Now that I was sober, real life threatened to come crashing down on me again—all the fears, all the worries, all the problems and mysteries I couldn't do anything about until daylight returned. Rans' remark about the neighbors not being able to hear me scream replayed in my mind, making me shiver with anticipation regarding the kinds of things he might do to me if given free rein.

He held himself above me on hard-muscled arms. Beyond the window, clouds sculled across the moon, dimming its light and blurring the details of his features into grayness broken only by the shining blue of his eyes.

"Hmm," he mused. "Let me see, now. A freshly unearthed voyeurism kink and a desire to lose control. You know, *I don't care* that you were draining their life force. Your exes were barmy not to stick around longer, luv."

I wrinkled my nose at him, not sure if he could see the expression in the deeper darkness that had overtaken the room. The huff of low laughter seemed to indicate that he could.

"Don't move a muscle," he warned. "I just need to grab something. Back in a tick."

With that, he kissed me quickly on the lips and rolled off the bed. I lay still, heart pounding with anticipation. As promised, he took only a moment.

"What is it?" I asked breathlessly, unable to make out detail now that the moon was hidden behind clouds.

The lamp switch clicked, casting a circle of warm light outward from the bedside table. It threw the planes of Rans' body into gold-limned dips and shadows, distracting me for a moment from the object dangling from his hand—a braided leather belt, the free end threaded through the buckle to form a small loop at the bottom.

"Give me your wrists, Zorah."

I didn't even think before I extended my wrists, feeling blood thrumming through every vein as my heart galloped wildly. Rans gathered my hands together, pressing his lips to the knuckles of first one, and then the other. He slipped the loop over them and tugged it closed, pressing my palms together as if in prayer. Leaning forward, he drew my arms over my head and tied the loose tail of the belt around one of the spindles in the headboard.

When he was done, he straightened and looked down at me with a serious expression. "The buckle isn't clasped," he said. "You can pull and struggle against it as much as you like, and it should hold, but if you really want to get loose, all you need to do is press your wrists apart to open up the loop so you can slide your hands out. Try it."

I tugged against the belt, first lightly, then harder until I could feel the soft leather biting into my wrists. Then I relaxed and wriggled my hands back and forth, feeling the loop widen as the buckle slid along the leather. I nodded, confident that I could easily slip my hands free if I needed to.

"And if you don't like something?" he asked, still regarding me seriously.

"I'll tell you to stop," I said in a breathy voice.

He smiled, letting his gaze slide down the length of my body like a caress. My nipples hardened, the points visible through the silky black material of my nightgown.

"So lovely, stretched out and on display for me like this," he murmured, brushing a fingertip over the nearest breast—the barest suggestion of a touch.

An electric tingle zapped from my nipple straight to my clit, and I caught my breath as a pulse of wetness soaked my inner thighs. Rans' nostrils flared, and a flush of heat rose from my neck to my cheeks—hopefully hidden by my dusky complexion.

Or maybe not.

"You're blushing," he teased. "And you're wet for me after a single touch? Succubi everywhere would be proud of you."

"Fucker," I said. I made a show of tugging and squirming against the belt, in hopes that it would hide the way I was rubbing my thighs together in an attempt to ease the pressure between them.

"Still blushing," he said, amused. "How far down does that flush go, I wonder? A pity all of that black silk is in my way—makes it hard to tell." A strong, callused hand slid over the silky material from breast to hip, igniting every nerve along the way.

I jerked against my bonds again for good measure. "Too bad you didn't think of that earlier," I taunted, already enjoying this new game. "It's going to be impossible to get it off me now, with my wrists tied like this."

Shit. Where had this kind of sex been all my life? My skin felt too tight, my body hot and needy and ready to be filled—all this from only a few minutes of teasing and play-acting.

The smile on Rans' face grew predatory, something about it sending a new pulse of urgency to my throbbing clit.

"Oh," he said, drawing out the word, "I don't need to untie you to get this flimsy scrap of cloth out of my way, little vixen."

"No?" I asked, breathless.

"No," he confirmed. His hands grasped either side of the plunging v-neck that displayed my cleavage, and the silky fabric ripped to my navel. My breasts spilled out, bare to his burning gaze. "Much better," he murmured.

"*Jesus, Mary, and Joseph,*" I cursed, my body on fire with the need to be touched. Taken. *Used.*

"Blasphemy. Zorah?" Rans accused, mock-appalled. "I'm *shocked.*"

"You're the one who told me I was part demon," I gasped. "You've got no one to blame but yourself. Now, *touch me,* goddamn it!" I writhed against the restraint for good measure.

He laughed, arranging his body in an elegant sprawl near the edge of the bed—giving me a clear view of his erect cock, but too far away for me to touch him, bound as I was. "No," he said, "I don't believe I will just yet."

I made a sound of frustration and struggled harder as he leaned casually on an elbow, only to freeze in place when he started stroking himself again, my eyes zeroing in on that slow slide of hand over dick. I could *feel* it… feel the steady rise of his lust flowing between us. I wanted that cock. I *ached* for it. Hell, I was practically salivating for it.

"Mmm," he hummed. "Edging. Never really saw the point until now. Nice to know you can still learn something new after seven hundred years."

I had no fucking clue what he was rambling on about, and I didn't really care. His orgasm was approaching, I could feel it. So close, so close, and I'd be able to feel that delectable flood of pleasure washing over me… soaking in to fill up the empty places inside me. Any second now…

He stopped, his hand stilling on his twitching cock, squeezing the base as a bead of pre-come dripped from the tip. All of that lovely, pent-up energy wavered on the brink… and stayed pent up. I made a pitiful noise, straining toward him but unable to reach.

I could feel the promise of his release sliding away as he continued to clamp his fingers around the base of his erection, his imminent orgasm subsiding. I lay there, panting and shivery, until he started jacking off again, smearing the pre-come over the head of his dick to use as lube. I could feel that it was even better for him that way, and I held my breath as he brought himself back to the edge—

—only to stop again.

Over and over he teased me with the promise of his release, only to pull it away at the last instant. By the fourth or fifth time, I was struggling in earnest, cursing him both silently and aloud. As if he'd sensed that I was about five seconds away from getting my wrists free and jumping him, he released his cock with a low growl.

"*Christ*. There's only so much of that I can take while I'm watching you writhe around with your wrists tied to the headboard," he said.

"Good," I snarled, giving my wrists another jerk for good measure. "Now get over here and give me what I want, or I'll—"

Whatever threat I might've come up with, it was cut off in a gasp of ecstasy when he ripped my nightgown the rest of the way open and palmed my sex roughly. Shameless and desperate, I ground my clit against the heel of his hand. I was so wet it should have been embarrassing, but concerns like that had fled long ago before my overwhelming need for what Rans was offering.

Instead of teasing, he was trying to drown me in pleasure now, or so it seemed. Long fingers delved inside me—stretching and probing—looking for the place along the front wall of my passage that made me arch wildly off the bed. His thumb brushed my clit, and just like that, I was coming with the promised scream—a mindless, wild thing bucking beneath him.

"*Bloody fucking hell*, luv," he cursed, poised over me as his magic fingers drew out my release and urged me toward a second one without so much as a pause for me to get my breath back. "I'll give you what you need, don't worry. But first, you'll give me more of *this*."

I whimpered, tugging fitfully at the belt even though I was exactly where I wanted to be. The feeling of being trapped here, subjected to pleasure at Rans' whim was addicting, and we hadn't even gotten to the best part yet. I couldn't have remembered my own name at that point, much less rattled off a list of the things I was supposed to be worrying about. I was completely in the moment, inhabiting the present with no thought for anything except my body's shuddering response to Rans' touch.

"Don't stop," I begged, as those deft fingers wrung more and more pleasure from me until I thought I'd go mad. "Don't stop, don't stop, *don't stop...*"

Lips brushed my ear. "Stop? I could keep you here until you pass out from what I'm doing to you, Zorah. And when you came around, you'd find yourself still tied to the bed, still with my fingers inside you, driving you mad. Maybe I'd wake you up by sucking on your clit at the same time."

I moaned, trembled, and came even harder, my voice rising to a high-pitched keen. Rans chuckled.

"Like that idea, do you?" he asked, and nipped my earlobe. Lips brushed down the length of my throat and lower. He sucked on first one nipple, and then the other, drawing on the pebbled points before letting them pop free. "Well, then—far be it from me to disappoint..."

When his mouth reached my clit and latched onto it, my heels scrabbled at the bedclothes—trying to get closer? Trying to get away? I wasn't sure. When the next orgasm rolled over me, I went limp, the fight going out of me all at once. The room spun. Nothing existed except Rans' mouth on me; his fingers inside me.

"There's my sweet little vixen," he murmured against my folds, lapping gently at my oversensitive clit while his fingers continued to stroke over the place inside me that sent starbursts erupting behind my closed eyelids. "Now you can have what you want from me."

With a final kiss to my folds, he slipped his fingers free of my clutching passage and prowled up the length of my body until his hips were cradled between my legs. His hard cock found my opening and slid inside with a single, unforgiving thrust.

And… oh, god—*this.*

This was bliss. I needed nothing more from life at this moment than the feeling of our flesh joining—of his animus flowing into me. He reached above my head one-handed and tugged at the belt until it fell away from my wrists, freeing my arms to circle his back and hold tight. I had become a peaceful, empty vessel, free of all cares and worries, existing only to be filled up with this wonderful feeling.

In turn, I would empty Rans of his troubles as well, leaving us free to just *be*… for a little while, at least, until we both had to go back out into a world that didn't want either of our kinds to exist.

We rocked together for a very long time, pleasure cresting and waning like a slow tide. Until finally, my teeth brushed Rans' collarbone in a fleeting nip, and he groaned low, spilling into me. Giving me everything he had to give.

I held him close as he filled me up, trading his vital energy for a brief stretch of serenity—giving me what I needed to survive, in exchange for the lesser gift I could give him in return. After his shudders finally stilled, he rolled us over until I was draped over his body like a blanket. Together, we drifted into dreamless sleep.

Four

For some reason, it still surprised me to wake up and find that I wasn't alone. That Rans hadn't left as soon as I'd fallen asleep. This probably said something deep and psychologically disturbing about the way my brain worked.

Self-esteem, said the little voice in my head. *Try getting some, one of these days.*

After that initial jolt of surprise passed, I realized a couple of things.

One—I felt safe and protected, tangled up with Rans in a stranger's stolen bed. It was a feeling that sat oddly in my chest after a couple of decades spent with the knowledge that in the end, very few people in my life really cared all that much what happened to me.

Two—my body felt *fucking fantabulous*. Well, okay. It felt fucking fantabulous except for a distinct soreness between my thighs that I couldn't really bring myself to mind. Other than that, though, I was rested and pain-free.

And in terrible need of a shower. Unfortunately, while drifting off in a lover's arms after a night of wild sex might be great for the psyche, it ignored several practical problems related to hygiene.

Oh, well.

I lazed for a few more minutes anyway. At some point as I'd slept, my lower body had slid off Rans, though one of my legs was still draped between his. I was still using his chest for a pillow, though. With his upper body bare, it was harder to tell if I'd drooled on him this time, so I decided to pretend that I hadn't.

He seemed pretty far out of it. His stillness was kind of disconcerting until I realized that I was expecting his chest to rise and fall beneath me. Which, of course, it wasn't doing because he was a vampire, and didn't need to breathe.

No breathing, no heartbeat. And yet, I knew exactly how much life resided inside that still form. I'd felt it. Several times now, in fact.

True, it was borrowed life—taken from those whose blood he drank. And I probably should have pressed the issue of him drinking from me harder last night. It was pretty obvious that without the turbo boost from my succubus blood to offset it, sex with me had drained him pretty badly.

Or maybe that was what he'd wanted? After all, here he was—completely relaxed and seemingly oblivious to the world, long hours after we'd finished. I wasn't about to begrudge him that.

It was still early, judging by the golden light slanting through the window. Now that I was conscious, though, reality was starting to clamor for my attention again. I was wide awake now, practically brimming with the energy I'd stolen from the man beneath me. With slow movements, I extricated my body from his, pausing to press a kiss to his lips when he stirred.

"Shh," I whispered. "I'm just going for a shower. It's still early."

He settled back, and I slid off the bed. The spaghetti straps of my ripped nightgown were still looped around my shoulders, leaving the ruined garment hanging down my back like some sort of bizarre cape.

Super Slut, I thought, a flush of giddy heat rising at the memory. But, *shit,* I was apparently the granddaughter of a sex demon and I'd somehow bagged a seven-hundred-year-old vampire as a fuck buddy.

I was damn well going to own it.

I let the silky fabric slide down my arms and grabbed it in one hand. Totally ruined, as I'd suspected… and still worth every penny. I debated the merits of dragging the ripped nightgown around in my single piece of luggage, versus throwing it away in a stranger's house for them to find and wonder about later.

I shoved it in the suitcase. Apparently Super Slut still had a few issues to work through before flying her freak flag for the entire world to see.

To make up for it, I grabbed Rans' discarded shirt from yesterday off a chair in the corner of the room where he'd placed it. Fair was fair. He'd been responsible for the cruel and unusual treatment of my lingerie; his punishment was the loss of a shirt. I slipped it on, only bothering with a couple of buttons, and went to take that much-needed shower.

I returned dressed the same way—with the addition of clean underwear—to find Rans still asleep, although he had at least shifted position.

Filled with the need to do something even though it was stupidly early in the morning, I staked out an area of carpet between the bed and the door. The yoga routine relaxed my muscles and kept thoughts of my father and the danger we were facing from completely taking over my mind.

"Wait. You're wearing *knickers*?" came a rough, freshly woken voice from behind me. "*Seriously*? And things were shaping up so promisingly there for a few minutes."

I broke position, twisting out of my textbook downward dog to face him. He was leaning on an elbow, looking rumpled and thoroughly fucked. And… yeah, okay. It was a really, *really* good look for him.

"Are you ogling my ass while I'm trying to do yoga?" I asked, crossing my arms and playing at being offended.

He laughed. "Your arse is smashing, luv, but I was ogling the whole package." His expression grew proprietary. "Along with the fact that your package is currently wrapped in one of my shirts."

I gave him a sugary sweet smile. "Yes, well—someone seems to have destroyed the perfectly nice nightgown that I only bought a few days ago. With Guthrie's money, I might add."

"It was in my way," Rans said carelessly. He looked me up and down, a speculative expression crossing his face. "Tell me… were you ever trained in dance?"

My eyebrows drew together in confusion. "Not unless you count ballet when I was, like, seven," I said. "Why?"

"I'm trying to decide the best way to teach you to fight," he said, as though that wasn't a completely off-the-wall statement. "You have a dancer's build, and good flexibility. Classical dance is one possible avenue into the martial arts."

Were we really having this conversation? I stopped myself before saying something dismissive… or disbelieving. It would have been hella-useful to know how to fight when Caspian's goons had tried to drag me into his car. True, I'd already been near collapse that evening—but given what my life had become now, who was to say that I wouldn't need better self-defense skills in the future?

"Okay," I said slowly. "Well, I don't know that Mrs. Pepperdyne's beginning barre exercises are going to help much at this point, but I did take a couple of self-defense classes when I was a teenager."

Rans nodded, thoughtful. "That could be useful. Let me think about logistics. You should at least know some basic moves. That, combined with the power you demonstrated when you thought Alby was going to hurt us will keep you from being completely helpless the next time the Fae catch up to us."

My eyes widened. "I am not sucking sex energy out of random people who try to attack me!" I said, appalled.

He scoffed. "Oh, yes—much better to let yourself be taken by your enemies than to risk offending your delicate human sensibilities."

At that, I bristled. "I never asked to be involved in periodic fights for my life, Rans."

His face softened. "No. I don't suppose you did."

"Besides," I added, trying to lighten the mood, "Fae energy makes me feel itchy."

He let the argument go, and stretched. "Yes, they are a rather prickly lot, aren't they? But you should still learn to fight."

I let my eyes roam over lean muscle and sinew before reluctantly acknowledging reality. "I'll think about it. So, when can we go talk to these people who might be able to help find Dad?" I asked.

Rans cast a jaundiced eye at the sun outside, and covered a yawn. "I imagine they'll be available in an hour or two. I'll go take a shower and try to wake up."

He still looked pretty wiped out, and a twinge of guilt hit me.

"I drained you too much last night," I said. "You should have stopped me."

He snorted. "Stopped you? Are you mental? Don't fret, luv. It was... *good*. Dawn's just not a great time for vampires. I'll grab a bite when we're out and about later. It'll be fine."

"*Grab a bite*?" I echoed. "You're a real comedian, you know."

Rans flashed a crooked grin and rolled out of bed, pausing to drop a kiss on my forehead. "I've had centuries to perfect my act." He headed toward the door, shameless in his nakedness, only to pause at the threshold and look back at me. "And a word to the wise—unless you want me even more drained than I am now, you should probably be wearing something other than my shirt when I get back," he threw over his shoulder.

I hid my grin until after he'd disappeared into the hallway. A few moments later, the shower turned on. It was all so… *domestic*. I shook my head and returned to my yoga routine.

By the time Rans wandered into the kitchen some twenty minutes later, I was seated at the table with a bowl of cereal and milk. I gestured at him with my spoon.

"You know," I said, pausing to swallow, "I'm still half-expecting to have a massive food allergy reaction, but I'm doing this anyway based on your say-so. Do you have any idea how long it's been since I've had a bowl of cornflakes with milk?"

"I wasn't aware it was the sort of thing one marked on the calendar," he said, "but I seriously doubt any common human foods have the power to do you much damage when you're topped off on sexual energy."

"I'm going to eat cheesecake," I enthused, still pointing at him with the spoon. "*Chocolate* cheesecake. Just as soon as I can find some. That, and pizza. With ham and pineapple."

He looked mildly queasy. "Not at the same time, I hope."

I raised an eyebrow, suddenly curious. "Can you eat normal food?" I asked. "Or just blood and the occasional glass of merlot?"

He shrugged. "I *can*. That is to say, nothing horrible happens if I do. Not much point, though. It mostly tastes like sawdust to me now."

My face fell. "I'm sorry. That sucks."

A half-smile twitched at his mouth. "'Sucks'? And you call me the comedian. Really… more vampire jokes at this ungodly hour of the morning?"

I winced a bit and shook my head. "Purely unintentional, I assure you."

"As all the best puns are. Now, finish your frosted sawdust flakes and cow juice, so we can get going."

I nodded. "Okay. Going where, exactly?" I asked before returning to the bowl of sugarcoated cereal.

"To talk to the conspiracy theorists who run the *Weekly Oracle,*" he said.

My brow furrowed. "What's the *Weekly Oracle?*" I asked, making a half-assed attempt to cover my full mouth with one hand as I spoke.

"Underground newspaper," he replied. "We'll visit their office for a chat."

I swallowed and cleared my throat. "And how does an underground newspaper help with finding where my dad's been taken?"

"The thing about conspiracy theorists is that they often stumble onto valuable information without having the faintest clue what it really means," he said.

I hesitated. "I was one, you know. All my life, really."

He looked interested. "A conspiracy theorist?"

"Yes. In fact, I guess I've recently become even more of one, although it's faeries and demons now, rather than Illuminati and freemasons."

He huffed a breath that might have been a chuckle. "It hardly counts as a conspiracy theory when it's true."

I gave him a sour look. "And it's not paranoia when they really are out to get you," I shot back. "I've been telling myself that all week."

"Indeed it isn't," he agreed.

I spooned up the last of the soggy cornflakes and drained my glass of juice. "Right. So, are we coming back here afterward?"

"As it stands now, we will," he said. "It's a good base of operations."

"But that could change if someone notices us while we're out and about," I hazarded. "Got it."

Rans nodded agreement. "Exactly. Shall we go?"

I looked at my dirty dishes, not wanting to risk Tom and Glynda returning to find someone else's milk dregs congealing in their sink if we ended up having to bug out. "Let me clean up first. No reason to be the worst house sitters ever."

He turned an amused eye on me. "When it comes to house sitters, you get what you pay for. And we're not being paid."

"We also hypnotized the homeowners into needing house sitters in the first place," I pointed out. "Come on—it's only a juice glass and a cereal bowl. I'll wash. You can dry."

The offices of the *Weekly Oracle* were about what you'd expect for an underground conspiracy rag.

Rans parked Glynda's Ford Focus a few blocks away. We walked along the breezy Chicago streets, discarded plastic bags and other trash blowing around us in a dizzying aerial ballet.

The building that housed the newspaper wasn't derelict, precisely, but it was pretty obvious that the objects of our interest weren't paying high-dollar rent on the place, either. Some of the windows on the ground level were boarded up, and efforts to paint over the ubiquitous graffiti tags on the walls appeared to be few and far between.

There was a small sign hanging over the only door that didn't have a "No Entry" sign plastered across it. An arrow indicated that the paper's offices were in the basement.

"Underground newspaper," I quipped. "Right."

"Some clichés are clichés for a reason," Rans said, opening the door and ushering me inside.

I was more than a little skeptical of what these people were likely to be able to do for us, but I also knew painfully well that I was out of my depth. It wasn't as though I had a ready-made list of suspects to question about my father's whereabouts.

The usual avenues—the normal things you were supposed to do when someone went missing—were no longer available to me. Calling the cops would be the same as standing under a flashing neon arrow saying, 'Come and get me, faeries!' I could try hiring a private investigator, but if I told them the truth about what was happening, they'd probably laugh in my face.

So, conspiracy theorists it was.

We trekked down a utilitarian stairwell that opened into a cavernous, mostly unfinished space. Some effort had been made to divide it into different areas using battered beige screens of the type designed for cubicle walls. The part that made up the front office area had a large receptionist desk acting as a symbolic barrier to keep walk-ins from wandering further back. From the depths of the basement space, the sounds of a printing press could be heard.

At first, I thought no one was around, but then I saw movement in the back.

"Just a second!" someone yelled, the words nearly drowned out by the noise of machinery.

Rans wandered over and leaned his elbows on the reception desk, while I looked around with interest. It really was exactly what I would have pictured if someone had asked me to imagine such a place. Empty takeout boxes littered many of the available surfaces, fighting for space with computer monitors, keyboards, and PC towers that looked like they'd been picked up cheap from a university rummage sale. Cables twisted through the irregularly lit space like spaghetti.

A red-haired guy in his early twenties made his way up to the front where we were waiting. He was clean-cut and well built. Frankly, I thought he would have looked more at home playing college football somewhere than rattling around in this place. Still, it was clear enough that he belonged here, based on the practiced way he avoided the bundles of computer cords snaking along the floor.

"Sorry about that," he said when he reached us. "What can I do for you?"

"I spoke with Derrick yesterday about getting some EMF readings from local hotspots," Rans said, and I perked up with interest.

"Oh, sure," the redhead replied. "You're *that* guy. Hang on a sec, I'll get him for you. In fact, why don't you come on back and sit down. He's just finishing up with replacing a busted piston on the inserter. Watch your step..."

We followed the guy as he gestured us to come around the reception desk. He led us to a desk that was more or less free of empty Chinese food containers, probably because the antiquated cathode ray computer monitor that was sitting on it took up most of the available space. There were a couple of cheap office chairs next to it. I sat down, while Rans continued to stand.

When the guy left to retrieve his friend, I leaned toward Rans and spoke out of the side of my mouth. "EMF readings? Like ghost-hunters use? Why?" I asked.

"You'll see soon enough," he replied unhelpfully.

I looked around the echoing basement full of outdated tech and rumbling machinery. "How on earth did you even find these guys?"

"Paranormal and conspiracy forums online, of course," Rans said, as if it were obvious. "Where else?"

Five

Anything I might have said was cut off by the arrival of a blond guy with thick-rimmed glasses and a smudge of grease on his cheek. He was attractive in a geeky sort of way—probably about my age, with gray eyes and a slender frame. He tilted his chin in greeting as he approached, wiping his hands on a dirty rag before tossing it onto the corner of the desk.

"Hey, man," he said. "I wasn't sure when to expect you back. Got those readings for you last night, though." His eyes flickered to me, an awkward smile tilting the corners of his broad mouth for only an instant before his gaze darted away.

Shy, I diagnosed. It was honestly a bit charming.

"Wonderful," Rans replied. "But where are my manners? JoAnne Reynolds, this is Derrick Nicolaev, better known in online circles as Hypnos. Derrick, JoAnne."

No doubt I should have been focusing on the fact that we were using the fake identities Guthrie had obtained for us, but my thoughts had crashed to a standstill.

"Wait, what?" I asked, aware that my eyes were about to pop out of my head. "*You're Hypnos*? Oh my god—I read all of your papers about government cover-ups of paranormal encounters on the Third Eye forum before it shut down!"

Rans was giving me a look somewhere between curiosity and bewilderment, probably because I was enthusiastically fangirling a geeky guy I'd just met in the basement of a boarded-up office building. It wasn't enough to stop me, though, as memories of those late night online forum discussions flooded me with nostalgia for a simpler time, before my life had turned into a bad SyFy Channel made-for-TV movie.

"You might not remember it, but we chatted a couple of times," I blathered, my mouth flapping onward without stopping to check in with my brain first. "About the connection between political violence and instances of paranormal sightings?" I gestured to myself. "I'm TeamEdward4eva. That was my username, I mean."

Hypnos—or rather, Derrick—looked a bit dazed by my outpouring, but to his credit he paused, obviously thinking back to that time several years ago when Third Eye had been a huge deal in online circles. Meanwhile, Rans looked like he was trying very hard not to collapse into screaming fits of laughter, so I glared at him.

"Oh, hang on." Derrick pointed a finger at me. "You were the girl whose mother got shot, right? The... state senator, wasn't it?"

Close. I didn't correct him, realizing now that it might not be a great idea for him to know exactly who he was talking to. Especially since Rans had just given him a fake name.

"Yeah," I said, glossing it over and moving on. "Wow. Small world, huh? So, you run a newspaper now?"

Derrick looked around and gave a self-deprecating little shrug. "If you can call it that. We have a pretty decent online presence, but we keep the lights on with advertising revenue from the dead-tree version. Enough about me, though. You're getting into the ghost-hunting business these days, huh?"

I cocked an eyebrow. "Apparently so," I said, trying to keep my tone neutral since I actually had no freaking clue why we were here.

"Cool," he said. "Turns out you picked a good place for it. Let me get the others up here and we'll show you what we've got." He turned toward the back, where the press had just begun to power down, rumbling into silence. "Yo—Isaac! Óliver!"

The redhead—Isaac, I was assuming—returned with another man following behind. The third member of the *Weekly Oracle* crew was a tough-looking Hispanic guy with shoulder-length black hair. My eyes fell to the empty left sleeve of his shirt, and I quickly dragged them back up, not wanting to stare. Something about his bearing made me think ex-military, and I wondered if he'd lost his arm in combat somewhere.

"You're the ones after the EMF data?" he asked, a faint Mexican or Central American accent coloring his voice.

"Yep," Rans agreed. "That's us."

Óliver nodded and pulled the remaining chair around to the front of the desk. "D, did you get all that shit plotted on the map last night?"

Derrick leaned on the edge of the desk. "Yeah, it's in the file dated yesterday. The pattern looked pretty clear."

"Pattern?" I asked as Óliver pulled up the file. Everyone clustered around to look over his shoulder—me included.

It was Isaac who had pity on me. "We have EMF meters set up at a bunch of area hotspots that sit on the ley lines crisscrossing northern Illinois and Indiana. Sometimes, if you plot the times and locations of the readings, patterns emerge. Derrick has some theories about energy waves related to sunspots affecting the strength of trapped ghosts."

I shot a look at Rans, still utterly in the dark as to our purpose here. He'd hidden his amusement from earlier behind an unreadable poker face, however, and there were no clues to be found in his expression.

"Let me see it," he said, his focus on the screen.

Derrick pointed at the map that appeared. I recognized Chicago sitting on the bank of Lake Michigan, along with a portion of the two states around it. Several red dots of various sizes with timestamps hovering above them covered the visible area.

"The size of the dot indicates the magnitude of the highest readings in the last seventy-two hours, with the timestamp showing when the peak occurred," Derrick said, tracing a finger along an arc defined by the biggest dots.

It meant nothing to me, but Rans nodded. "Right. So the biggest power surges are all following that single ley line, heading from west to east at a high rate of speed."

"Weird," Isaac said. "Have there been any solar flares during that period?"

"No," Óliver grunted. "The last big one was six days ago."

"It doesn't do a damn thing for my pet theory," Derrick offered wryly, "but does it help you at all?"

Rans straightened and flashed him a charming smile. "Possibly so. Whatever the case, I appreciate the assistance, lads."

Derrick shrugged. "The data needed to be collated anyway. You want a printout or a file transfer of this?"

"No, no," Rans said. "Not necessary. I just needed to see the pattern."

Óliver looked up at him, raising an eyebrow. "You got a different theory about these readings? Because at this point, I'm open to just about anything."

Rans shook his head. "Not really. At least, not one I'm ready to air yet, but you know how it is. Every piece of data helps." He turned his attention back to me. "Perhaps we should leave these gentlemen to their work now. Ready to head out?"

I'm ready to get some freaking answers, I tried to project with my expression, but aloud, I only said, "Sure." I smiled at Derrick. "It was really great to run into you in meatspace, Hypnos. Keep on fighting the good fight, okay?"

I let my smile encompass the other two, as well. Derrick awkwardly shook my hand, while the others acknowledged me with brief nods. After a final brief farewell, Rans ushered me back up the stairwell and out the door leading onto the street.

"Care to explain all that?" I asked once we were outside.

"Certainly. First things first, though." He eyed me up and down, a very strange look on his handsome face. "'TeamEdward4eva,' Zorah? *Really*?"

I stared at him blankly for a beat before the implications registered. Heat flooded my cheeks.

"I was sixteen when I chose that username!" I protested. "It was a popular series—millions of people read it!"

He had that look again—the one that said he was battling back laughter only with extreme difficulty. "I swear, if the word sparkle passes your lips..."

"*Real women crave the sparkle,*" I muttered, casting a glare up at him. "That was my sig line."

A single bark of laughter escaped his control. "Bloody hell, luv." He shook his head. "Ah, well. It could be worse. If you'd been Team Jacob, you and I might be having a serious problem right now."

I narrowed my eyes. "I feel like I should point out that my being a teenage girl at the time excuses me for all of this. Whereas you're seven hundred years old, and you've clearly got strong opinions regarding a girly young-adult vampire story."

"Boredom is a powerful motivator," he said, before visibly wrestling his amusement back under control. "Now, though, we really do have other things to worry about."

I sobered, because yeah—that was putting it mildly. "So talk. Why do you care about ghost-hunting all of the sudden?"

"Because they aren't tracking ghosts. They're tracking Fae travel along the ley lines. They just don't realize it."

"Okay, explain that to me," I said. "The magic and ghost stuff was never really my thing, ironic as that now seems. Ley lines are supposed to be... like, energy highways, right?"

"In a way. Originally, humans became aware of them when several people noticed that large monuments and religious structures tended to be built along particular map lines, even though there was no coordination or purposeful planning to make it happen that way."

I frowned, mulling that over. "So... what? People built monuments in certain places because of invisible energy paths running through the area?"

Rans shrugged. "Theoretically. Depending on who's telling it, humans were either spontaneously drawn to the ley lines, or they were drawn to the concentrations of Fae nearby—since Fae use the lines for magical transportation across long distances."

My thoughts turned back to Albigard and his portals. "Oh. Is that how Tinkebell was able to whisk us from place to place?"

But he shook his head. "No. Alby is a powerful magical practitioner in his own right. Many Fae can fold local space to move short distances. The ley lines are for global travel."

I started to glimpse where he was going with this. "Meaning Fae were traveling along the line on that map we just saw, and this was happening around the time Dad disappeared. You think it's connected?"

"I had a theory," Rans said. "One that Derrick's data supports. The Fae tend not to travel back and forth from wherever they're stationed on Earth very often. There's no way to prove it conclusively, but the timing makes it likely they were transporting a high-level prisoner… or a high-level collaborator."

My throat went dry. "Transporting him where?" I rasped.

"To the Fae world of Dhuinne. The ley line you saw on the map leads directly across the Atlantic Ocean to County Meath in Ireland. And the weak spot between the two realms—the gate used to move between the worlds—is inside a burial mound on the Hill of Tara."

My brain didn't seem to want to work at the moment, but I forced myself to follow the logical steps he was laying out anyway. "Are you saying that my dad isn't on Earth anymore?" Even speaking the words aloud made me feel cold, despite the summer heat reflecting off the concrete.

His eyes cut to me, assessing my reaction. "I'm saying it's a possibility."

Jesus. If he was right, what was I supposed to do now? I swallowed hard.

"We should go visit the westernmost place where Derrick's equipment picked up high readings," I said, thinking it through as rationally as I could. "If they were traveling west to east, that should be the point they left from, shouldn't it? Maybe we can find more clues there."

Rans was still watching me. "You really want to traipse up to a Fae-controlled site and start asking questions, Zorah? Because if I'm right, Caspian's mates would be pleased as punch to whisk you away to join your father—and not for a touching family reunion."

The panicked feeling I'd been holding at bay for the last day or so was clamoring in my stomach, threatening to break loose and consume me. I was already a fugitive. Even with Rans protecting me for reasons I still couldn't claim to understand, realistically, how long was I going to be able to avoid the Fae? I couldn't just attach myself to Rans like a leech for the rest of my natural life, in hopes that he would continue to beat off my pursuers with a stick… or a sword.

"*What,* then?" I asked, hearing desperation seep into my voice.

I hadn't been joking, back at my dad's place. Right now, finding him was the only thing driving me forward. Even if I failed—even if my attempt resulted in my capture rather than his rescue—I still had to try. If I let my only remaining family member languish in my enemy's hands while I hid myself away like a terrified mouse in a hole, what kind of daughter did that make me? What kind of *person* did that make me?

"I thought we'd pass this new information to Alby and see what he can make of it," Rans said, looking at me as though he was weighing the likelihood of me losing my shit right here on the street. "He's better positioned than either of us to learn something useful, although I can always do a bit of quiet aerial reconnaissance on the place at night, if need be."

Right. Because my vampire lover could turn into mist and fly. *Fuck.* What had my life become?

"Do you really think we can trust him?" I asked, not much liking this plan. "Albigard, I mean?"

He paused, looking thoughtful. "There are... reasons why Albigard wants to stay on top of what's going on within the Unseelie Court. Those reasons are self-serving—but, these days, they're also in conflict with what most of the rest of his race wants. That makes him an ally in some respects, if not necessarily others."

"The enemy of my enemy is my friend?" I asked sourly.

"Until he isn't. Quite so."

"I really don't like this," I told him.

"I'd gathered," he said.

We'd covered maybe half the distance back to the car and were passing a small encampment of homeless people. They'd set up on the boundary of the rather derelict area where the *Weekly Oracle* kept their cheap basement offices and a busier area with open storefronts and foot traffic.

Rans glanced at the makeshift tents, and then at a fast food restaurant down the block. "Time for lunch, I think."

I glanced at the angle of the sun, thinking that it seemed awfully early. "More like brunch, I'd have thought."

"Brunch, then." He was rummaging in a pocket. A moment later, he came up with a couple of folded bills. With a jolt, I realized they were hundreds.

"I'm… not really all that hungry yet," I told him, eyeing the cash.

"As you like," he said. "I am, though. Someone seems to have sucked me dry last night, and I haven't had a chance to refill yet." He lifted my hand and pressed the money into it. "Do me a favor and get enough food for—" He broke off, glancing over the homeless encampment again. "—roughly a dozen people. Then bring it back here. Consider it your good deed for the day."

I opened my mouth, closed it, and then opened it again. "Are you about to drink blood from homeless people?"

"Yes, I am about to drink blood from homeless people, after which I will provide them with some spending money, along with a free meal for them and the rest of their compatriots." He raised a challenging eyebrow. "Does that offend you?"

I stood there for a minute, holding the breath I'd drawn to speak. "No," I decided. "Not so long as you don't drain them as badly as you drained me that first afternoon in St. Louis. Because… I'm sorry, Rans, but that *really sucked.*"

A grim little smile tipped up the corners of his mouth. "Last night with you was intense, luv—but not *quite* as intense as a shotgun blast through the chest. I'll try to mind my table manners."

I nodded, mostly satisfied by the reassurance, and started to turn away before another thought struck me. "Is it safe for me to, you know…" I gestured at the restaurant down the street.

"The Fae aren't watching the entire city around the clock. We're no place near your father's home, government offices, or any travel hubs. It's fine."

With that, he peeled away and approached a skinny kid who was lounging in front of one of the makeshift tarp tents. Rans crouched in front of him and after a brief conversation, the kid called to some of the others nearby. Rans shot a glance over his shoulder at me, as though wondering why I hadn't left to buy the food yet. His blue eyes were glowing.

I pivoted and marched down the street to buy hamburgers. Or possibly breakfast sandwiches if it was still too early for the lunch menu. Should this be bothering me more? I wasn't sure. The feeling in my chest might possibly have been distaste. It also might have been burning, territorial jealousy at the idea of Rans' lips closing over someone else's neck… his teeth piercing someone else's skin.

I stood in line, resolutely not examining the feeling any closer. When I reached the counter, I bought breakfast sandwiches and hash browns—muttering something under my breath about picking up food for the office when the cashier eyed the hundred dollar bills curiously.

When the order was finished I hauled the ridiculous, oversized bag back to where I'd left Rans. Apparently, the grisly part was already done, because he was lounging with casual equanimity against a wall, chatting with an old guy whose beard was stained yellow.

On the one hand, I had no particular desire to watch Rans drink blood from random people. But on the other hand, I had a vague impression that I was being *managed*. That he'd sent me away specifically so I wouldn't make a scene while he was doing the dirty deed. Or deeds, since I gathered he'd intended to drink from more than one. None of the people around him looked upset. Had he mesmerized them into forgetting what had happened? *Probably,* I thought, remembering those glowing eyes glancing back at me as I'd left.

More importantly, though, none of them looked weakened or debilitated. Maybe I shouldn't have worried. Rans had seven freaking centuries of practice at this, after all. I took a deep breath and strolled up.

"Hey," I said awkwardly. "Who wants breakfast sandwiches and hash browns?"

Within moments, I was the most popular person on the block—surrounded by people in thrift store clothing and ragged military surplus gear. They helped pass everything around, making sure everyone got a fair share.

Almost everyone, at least. When the crowd cleared, I noticed an elderly woman hanging back in the shadows. Her short, iron-gray hair stood up in wild wisps pointing every which way, and her cheeks had the sunken look that came from missing too many teeth.

"Hey, Alma," called the skinny kid Rans had been talking to when I left. "You okay back there? Come get some food."

But Alma only scowled at him.

Not wanting the poor old dear to miss out on a hot meal, I rummaged for the last container of hash browns and approached her, pasting on what I hoped was a non-threatening smile.

"Hey, Alma. I'm Zo—" I caught myself and substituted my fake name. "I'm JoAnne." God, I was still appallingly bad at this whole thing. I extended the styrofoam container. "I've got some hash browns left—"

The container and its contents went flying as Alma knocked it out of my hand with unexpected viciousness. I gaped at her in surprise as her lips peeled back, revealing gums populated by a few rotting teeth.

"*Demon girl!*" she hissed, pulling a makeshift blade out of her jacket and plunging it toward my face.

Six

I stumbled backward, but a hand appeared unexpectedly in my vision, catching the old woman's wrist in a grip like iron. She shrieked in Rans' face, her expression unhinged. Manic.

"Well, *bugger,*" Rans said as he caught her other arm, restraining her. "Maybe I should have expected something like this."

"Alma!" The skinny kid and a couple of other people were hurrying toward us, alarm clouding their faces.

I scrambled out of the way, feeling my heart thudding against my ribcage after the unexpected jolt of adrenaline. Rans twisted the shard of sharpened metal out of Alma's hand, and caught her again when she tried to go for his eyes with her nails.

"Jesus, Alma—what are you doing?" the kid cried, skidding to a stop in front of her. "You need to calm down… you're gonna bring the cops down on us!"

A fresh sliver of fear pierced me. My last couple of encounters with the cops had taught me that the old maxim, 'Always trust a policeman' didn't hold true when you were a fugitive succubus hybrid on the run from a bunch of pissed-off faeries. If law enforcement did show up, there was a damned good chance the Fae would find out I was here—and Rans, too.

"Filthy hell-spawn!" Alma was screeching. "*Abomination*!"

Rans' eyes pinned me. "Go to the car. She may calm down once you're out of sight." He rummaged in his pocket one-handed, the other hand still holding Alma's wrists trapped. Keys arced through the air across the short distance separating us, followed by his phone. I caught both items as he spoke again. "I'll take care of this. If I don't catch up to you in ten minutes, call A.C. from the contact list and let him know what's happening. A.C. is for Atlantic City… got it?"

"G-got it," I stammered, realizing that must mean Nigellus.

"I'm really sorry, ma'am," said the skinny kid. "Not sure what's gotten into her. She's been pretty calm lately, for the most part."

"It's okay," I managed, and fled.

I tried not to look like someone who was expecting rogue police officers to descend in force with handcuffs and truncheons. I tried not to feel like it was St. Louis all over again. I made it to Glynda's Ford Focus and opened the driver's side door with shaking hands, sliding inside and slamming it behind me before clicking the locks shut.

Heart still galloping, I started the engine, adjusting the seat and mirrors just in case I had to move fast. In between checking every few seconds for approaching red and blue lights, I pulled Rans' phone out and unlocked it, scrolling through the contact list. A.C. was there, as was Guthrie, under his own name. Further down was an entry called 'Tink.' Albigard, I was willing to bet.

I checked my surroundings again, while also keeping an eye on the time.

It occurred to me that I should add these numbers to my burner phones, in case I ever needed them and didn't have access to his. I was still carrying one of the cell phones I'd bought in St. Louis; the other was packed in my luggage in the trunk. Pulling it out of my pocket, I tapped in the three contacts I thought I'd recognized, plus Rans' number.

Seven minutes had passed since I started the car. There was still no sign of any police arriving… and now a familiar figure was approaching along the sidewalk. I breathed a sigh of relief. Rans looked like he was out for a casual stroll—completely unconcerned. I unlocked the doors as he approached, and he eased himself into the passenger seat.

"Deep breath, luv," he said. "I'm ninety-nine percent certain that my attempt at damage control was successful. Well… ninety percent." He paused. "Definitely more than eighty-five percent. Anyway, I'm sorry about all that. I should've considered that the Fae might be utilizing the homeless and mentally ill as watchdogs in the city."

I handed him his phone, and he pocketed it.

"Tell me exactly what happened back there," I said, striving to keep my tone calm.

Rans scrubbed a hand through his hair. "Fae can influence humans, as you've already seen with the police both here and in St. Louis," he said.

"I know," I replied, thinking of the behavior of Daisy and the other board members at MMHA. "Caspian got his claws into some of my coworkers back home."

He nodded. "I'm not surprised. Chances are, they'll have returned to normal now that he's not breathing down their necks—though it's possible he will have kept someone under his thrall to let him know on the off chance you decide to go back there."

I thought of Vonnie… of Daisy. A shiver chased its way up my spine.

"It takes a lot of energy to hold onto a healthy human mind for an extended period," he continued. "But it's easier to implant a compulsion into someone with a mental illness. At a guess, our friend back there suffers from schizophrenia. These days, I imagine the voices are telling her to attack anyone who feels like a demon. No doubt her Fae handler implanted a sensitivity to demon animus in her mind, as well."

Now I felt sick. "And are the voices also telling her to report back to the Fae if she finds any demons?"

"I expect so," Rans said. "Which is why I attempted to influence her to forget what she'd just seen."

"That's what you meant by damage control?"

"Yes."

"Damage control that you're eighty-five percent certain was successful?" I prodded.

"Yes." He cleared his throat. "Well, eighty percent, anyway. Overcoming Fae influence is tricky. I'm fairly certain it worked, though."

I swallowed a sigh. "Is it safe to go back to the house?"

"We'll drive around for an hour or two. Make sure no one's tailing us. If they aren't, there's no reason not to return." He stretched in his seat, vertebrae popping audibly as he continued. "After all, our house sitting contract isn't up until tomorrow. Hate to shirk on the job."

I checked traffic in the mirror and eased out of the parking spot. "All right. Driving around randomly for an hour it is, then," I said. "Let me know if anyone's following us, so I'll know when to panic."

"Oh, I will," he said, with a tone of relish that I didn't really appreciate. "How are your high-speed driving skills? I haven't been in a good car chase since—"

"Three days ago?" I finished, thinking back to that horrible night in St. Louis.

Rans made a dismissive noise. "Pfft. That was a motorcycle chase, not a car chase. And it hardly qualified as a *good* one. With that silver knife sticking out of my shoulder, I barely enjoyed it all."

"You are certifiably insane," I said, carefully obeying all relevant traffic laws as I turned left onto a random street.

He let out a soft snort and didn't try to deny it. The silence stretched as I drove through the unfamiliar city with no destination in mind. As I thought over everything I'd learned, another question occurred.

"It must have been pretty difficult for Caspian and Albigard to influence all those cops," I said, remembering the police swarming the bus station, not to mention the ones waiting for us at O'Hare yesterday.

"Indeed so," Rans agreed. "Though I've suspected for a long time that the Fae single out members of law enforcement who are... shall we say, on the less stable side. PTSD, anxiety, addiction problems, borderline personality disorder—those types of things would make them more vulnerable to Fae influence. But even so, it was a startling display of blunt force on both occasions."

"Should I be flattered?" I grumbled. "Because I don't feel flattered."

"Let's just say, you seem to be a very popular individual among the inhuman crowd."

I shot him a brief glance before returning my attention to traffic.

"Including you," I said flatly. "Although I still don't claim to understand why."

It would be way too easy to fall into the fairy-tale princess narrative with this man. This *vampire.* He'd ridden to my rescue, saving me from a fate worse than death. I'd cradled his body against mine... taken him apart, and been taken apart by him in return. All of it had felt so goddamned *right.*

But a seven-hundred-year-old vampire did not fall for a twenty-six-year-old mostly human waitress just because her succubus-tainted blood acted like Viagra for the undead. There was more to this story, and until I learned it, I needed to keep my head on straight. Faeries might be real, but fairytale endings sure as hell weren't. I'd learned that lesson at the tender age of six.

Rans regarded me for a long moment. "There are reasons why the Fae are so fixated on you, and I don't know yet what all of those reasons are."

I scowled. "I thought it was because Grandpa Demon shit all over the Big Important Peace Treaty by knocking up a human woman on the sly. And because my mom somehow managed to get pregnant with me, in turn."

"Then why not just kill you?" Rans asked. "It wouldn't have been difficult, and it isn't as though they lack practice at it."

My head whipped around so fast that the car swerved in its lane before I corrected it. "Wait. Are you saying you think the Fae were responsible for killing my mother?"

Snippets of conversation and memory slotted into place in my mind like puzzle pieces. Fae found it easier to control the mentally ill. My mother's assassin had been mentally ill. He'd scrawled 'Kill the demons' on his cell wall in blood, the night he'd hung himself.

"Oh, yes—almost certainly," Rans said, breaking through my moment of revelation.

I swallowed hard. "The forensics report said that the hollow-point rifle round the gunman used had been filled with salt. Do you know why that was?"

"Full-blooded demons are functionally immortal," Rans told me, "but their bodies are vulnerable to salt. It burns them, and enough of it can incapacitate them completely, at least for a time. From what I know of cambions like your mother, the salt was probably an unnecessary embellishment. The bullet alone would have sufficed. It's inclusion does, however, imply more knowledge and preparation than your average demon-fearing religious lunatic might be expected to employ."

My hands gripped the steering wheel so tightly that the knuckles turned white. "So I've been right, all this time. There was more to my mother's death than a random lunatic's delusions."

"Far more, yes," Rans confirmed.

Vindication should have felt better than this.

"Doesn't really help, does it?" Rans asked, eerily perceptive.

"Ask me again after I've got Dad back, and when no one is trying to kidnap or kill me," I said at length.

Rans did not reply.

I refused to acknowledge the little voice in my head that whispered, *And when will that be?*

Ninety minutes later, I pulled into Tom and Glynda's garage. There was no indication that anyone had attempted to follow us, though Rans had even gone so far as to direct me out of the city to a heavily wooded area that would confuse any potential aerial surveillance.

I might not have been hungry when I'd picked up food for Rans' blood donors earlier, but my stomach was rumbling audibly by the time we entered the deserted house.

"Pizza," I declared without preamble. "I am totally ordering a pizza right now."

If I was going to end up being hunted for the rest of my tragically short life, I was damn well taking advantage of my apparent physical recovery while I could. Pizza was an autoimmune dieter's nightmare—dairy and nightshade sauce served on a gluten-y crust. And I was going to eat an entire Hawaiian one just as soon as a delivery driver could get it here.

"If it involves pineapple, I don't want to hear about it," Rans said with clear distaste. "But yes, you might as well. You'll need the calories for later."

I eyed him warily. "Why? What happens later?"

His quick grin was the slightly unhinged one I'd seen on a few occasions before. "Training, of course. Had you forgotten?"

Between the day's revelations and the small matter of a random old woman attempting to plunge a knife through my eye, I certainly *had* forgotten about his musings this morning regarding self-defense training.

"Oh," I said. "That. Okay."

It wasn't that I didn't have misgivings. I did. But I also had a body that—for the first time in years—felt strong and vital. Part of me was intrigued to find out what I could do with it.

"Order your disgusting fruit-on-a-pizza while I talk to Albigard," Rans said. "Or while I leave a message for Albigard, at least. The useless sod is probably nowhere near his phone right now."

I frowned as I hunted for a phonebook, since the cheap flip-phones I'd bought were no good for internet searches. "What do you mean? Doesn't he have a cell?"

"He's Fae," Rans said, as though that explained anything. "Their magic is hard on tech. The irritating twat has an analog landline with a remote voicemail service that mostly works... when he can be bothered to answer it or check messages."

I raised my eyebrows, remembering the fried clock display in his Mercedes. It hadn't just been flashing twelve; it had been completely scrambled. The car looked like an older model, too—perfectly restored and maintained, certainly, but I wondered now if that was because newer models relied so heavily on computerized components.

"Mind you," Rans continued, "the upside is that Fae are rubbish at electronic surveillance. Not that they can't get humans to do it for them, but in general it means that you won't find them tapping phone lines or using technological tracking devices on cars. It's just not the way their minds work. They're more likely to use spells."

"And yet you got us fake ID and credit cards," I pointed out. "And you wouldn't let me call Dad for fear they'd find out."

"That's different," he said. "They've got human law enforcement involved in their attempts to track you down. But while Albigard may be out of favor with the Unseelie Court, they're hardly going to sic human police or private investigators on him in the normal course of things."

I shrugged. "If you say so. I'm calling for that pizza now. I'd ask if you wanted anything, but I don't think they carry merlot. Or plasma, for that matter."

"Pity," he said, and went to the next room to place his call so we wouldn't be talking over each other.

The pizza arrived thirty-five minutes later, and was every bit as good as my appetite had insisted it would be. Rans watched me eat it with something between fascination and disgust, raising an eyebrow at the nearly orgasmic noises I was making.

He'd ended up leaving a message for Albigard, who wasn't picking up his phone. I chafed at the delay in moving forward with finding out where Dad was and how I could get him back, but Rans convinced me to give it until evening, when Albigard was more likely to get the phone message.

After allowing me a scant hour for my late lunch to settle, he chivvied me into clothing suitable for a workout and dragged me to the downstairs family room.

"I can't believe you hypnotized the homeowners to leave, and now you're *moving their furniture,*" I said, trying not to stare as he pulled a large sofa off to the side with inhuman strength.

"It's in my way," he said with a faintly predatory smile that reminded me he'd said the same thing about my nightgown last night. I supposed that meant I should be glad he was *moving* the furniture instead of breaking it into pieces and tossing it aside.

"Now what?" I asked, looking at the empty space he'd cleared.

"Now," he said, "You show me what all that yoga has done for your range of flexibility." He reached around to the small of his back and pulled out a short dagger. "And afterward, I'll show you how to use *this*."

Seven

I stared at the dark metal knife blade. "How the hell did you get that? You said you didn't bring any weapons to Chicago—"

"Because my contact here could provide them," he finished.

"Your *contact* arrested us on sight!" I said.

"And before he cut us loose, he added a few essentials to our luggage." Rans tilted the blade back and forth beneath the family room's overhead lights.

I examined it, still unable to wrap my head around the relationship between Rans and Albigard. "Why is it so tarnished?" I asked.

"It's not," he replied. "Iron blades are always that color."

Iron? That was the second knife I'd seen in the past few days made of an unusual material.

"What is it with Fae and weird metals?" I asked, reaching a careful finger out to run along the flat of the blade.

Rans huffed a breath of amusement. "Silver for vampires. Salt for demons. Iron for Fae. Earth metals interfere with their magical core—their connection to Dhuinne."

My brow furrowed. "So Albigard gave you weapons that could hurt him and the other Fae?"

"As I told you," Rans said, removing the sheath that had nestled at the small of his back and sliding the knife into it, "Alby's aims don't really align with most of his people's aims these days."

"Apparently not." I took a breath and let it go for now. "All right. So... yoga? I should warn you, I'm not used to having an audience."

One corner of his mouth twitched up. "Who said anything about an audience?"

I raised both eyebrows as he set the sheathed knife and his cell phone aside before unbuttoning his shirt. He wore a dark tank top beneath, exposing the abstract tribal pattern of his tattoos against the pale skin of his right arm. His belt, shoes, and socks followed, and okay, yeah—I was totally staring now.

The look he shot me was mock-severe. "Focus, luv. Mirror me now—back to back."

He guided me down into a sukhasana pose—vertebrae stacked, legs crossed, wrists resting on knees. I could feel him take up the same pose behind me, and a little flutter began low in my stomach as our bodies relaxed into each other, spine to spine. Our difference in height meant that the back of my head fit into the curve of his nape.

"You're breathing," I realized, feeling the expansion of his ribs fall into sync with my own steady in-and-out.

"It's yoga," he said, sounding amused. "Breathing is rather the point, isn't it? Now, stop talking and match me."

The muscles in his shoulders flexed, and I saw his arms stretch straight out to the sides in my peripheral vision. Entranced, I matched his movement, and cool fingers twined with mine. He used the light grip to lead me through a series of basic stretches. My body melted into his as he lifted our joined hands straight up, putting gentle traction on my spine until it popped and eased.

Next he stretched my body to first one side, then the other, opening my ribcage. A gentle side-to-side twist at the waist followed. Then he leaned forward into a modified child's pose, bowed over his crossed legs, my spine arched over his as I leaned back to maintain the contact between us.

"Very nice," he said as he straightened, releasing my wrists with a slow caress. "Now turn around."

I almost didn't want to. What we were doing shouldn't feel so intimate. My body was giving itself over to him, leaning on his strength in a way that seemed at odds with my mind's insistence on maintaining my distance… on protecting myself.

But he was already rearranging us face-to-face, helping me stretch into a forward bend, deepening it further with a steady pull on my wrists, which I returned, keeping us in balance. Gradually, the poses grew more challenging and complex, testing my range of movement and core fitness.

I already knew that Rans' lean-muscled body held a startling strength, but I hadn't appreciated before how effortlessly controlled that strength could be. He lay on his back beneath me, legs straight at a right angle to his body, supporting me in a perfect folding leaf posture above him. No part of me touched the ground; instead, I hung perfectly balanced over the platform of his feet, which were pressing into the creases of my hips to support me.

A low throb had taken up residence between my thighs sometime earlier, competing with whatever complicated thing my heart was trying to do. I didn't like the combined feeling… and I also craved it like a drug I hadn't known I needed. Strong hands slid down my shoulders, brushing along the length of my arms and guiding me into a new pose that stretched my spine between the grip he now held on my wrists and the fulcrum of my hips resting on his feet.

And—holy Jesus *fuck*–it felt good. Not just because of the deep stretch through my pelvis and back, but also for the feeling of flying… of being suspended above the earth like a bird on the wing. A faint moan slipped out on my next exhalation, and his grip on my wrists tightened, his thumb caressing my pulse point.

I knew I shouldn't be doing this. I shouldn't be letting these walls crack, because I wasn't at all sure what sort of monsters lay in wait behind them. As though sensing that I was in danger of being overwhelmed, Rans completed the pose and helped me dismount, my feet landing lightly on the carpet as he bent his knees and stiff-armed my upper body into an upright position.

I took a step back, my breathing going ragged as he relaxed back, lacing his fingers across his chest and looking up at me from the floor with depthless blue eyes.

"I, uh, need to use the bathroom," I stammered, and fled the room.

A few moments later, I closed the upstairs bathroom door behind me and leaned on it. My eyes were burning and I didn't even know *why*.

Shit, shit, shit.

Was I so pathetically desperate for some kind of intimacy in my life that I was going to have a meltdown after a goddamned *yoga session*? Rans needed me to help him figure out what the Fae were up to, and I needed him for the protection he could offer.

Okay, so we'd fucked a few times. I was part succubus. I needed sex, and he knew that. He seemed to get enjoyment and a bit of temporary mental peace out of it, so it was a mutually beneficial arrangement. That was all. Anything else was just my loneliness reading things into a purely practical partnership. Things that *weren't there*.

My heart was pounding again. I had to start thinking about how to extricate myself from all of this. I needed to get my dad, and then I needed to get out. The Fae would never stop chasing me. Eventually they'd track me down again. Hell, if Rans hadn't been successful in overcoming Alma's conditioning and making her forget about me, they might well know already that I was in Chicago.

If they descended *en masse* and Rans tried to protect me… well, I'd seen him fight off a few Fae, but now I also knew that the Fae had a weapon that could murder vampires. I absolutely refused to be the reason he died.

I took a deep breath and let it out slowly. I had already agreed to giving Albigard a few hours to get the phone message and start looking into things. Since I was the Fae's real target, it wouldn't make any sense for them to hurt Dad, or… kill him.

No sense at all. They probably intended to use him as some sort of hostage against me, right? There was still time to save him.

And now all I had to do was go back downstairs to the family room and pretend I hadn't just come close to sniveling like a little girl because someone finally cared enough about me to do all the things Rans was doing. Because I'd finally found someone who *fit* inside my messed-up life.

I thumped my head gently against the door a couple of times, in the vain hope that it would make my brain stop being stupid. Then I flushed the toilet and ran the water in the sink to support my paper-thin excuse for running off.

When I returned, Rans was waiting, leaning against the foot of the couch in an easy sprawl. "All set," I said, too brightly. "What's next?"

Rans shot me an enigmatic glance from beneath his dark fringe of hair. "Next? Why, Zorah…I'm *so* glad you asked…"

Four hours later, I was a sweating, shaky mess after an afternoon spent going over and over basic self-defense moves. Maybe Rans had sensed my inability to cope with gentleness, or maybe this was simply the usual way you taught someone how to fight. Whatever the case, my gooey, doe-eyed emotions had been replaced first by surprise, then frustration at being overpowered again and again by a much larger and stronger opponent… and finally by sheer exhaustion.

I didn't feel that I'd made any significant amount of progress in my skill set, but there *had* been a couple of occasions before my fatigue started to overcome me where our sparring fell into a sort of rhythm, almost like a dance. The feeling lasted for only a few seconds each time, at which point Rans would duck through my guard and subdue me.

As far as the iron dagger went, we hadn't progressed beyond him showing me how to grip the hilt properly, and a few minutes of practice at drawing it from its sheath at the small of my back. At the moment, if I tried to use it, I'd be more likely to injure my opponent by accident than on purpose… if I didn't fall over my own feet and stab myself to death instead, that is.

Rans leaned against a bare stretch of wall, not even winded. There wasn't a drop of sweat on the smug bastard's body, either.

"I thought you said you'd taken self-defense classes?" he asked.

Hmm… maybe I could try *throwing* the knife at him?

"I knew enough…" I said around wheezing gasps, "to get away… when Caspian grabbed me at the restaurant."

He made a dismissive noise. "Golden Boy was just trying to rattle you. He wanted to get a feel for your power levels, and your experience."

"Well, it fucking worked," I grumbled, my heart rate gradually slowing to normal. I used the hem of my shirt to blot sweat from my face—something that might have been more effective if the fabric wasn't already as sweat-soaked as the rest of me.

"Drink some water," Rans said without bothering to move from his position propping up the wall. "Then take a shower. Do you want me to join you for that part?"

I stilled, trying to pick through that sentence for the underlying meaning. People just... didn't say shit like that to me.

"Why?" I ended up asking, since mindreading skills were failing me.

His expression was two parts exasperated and one part pitying. "In case you need to feed from me," he said patiently.

The unexpected jolt that hit me in the belly was unwelcome. Damn it, I was trying to pull away, not get entangled further in the web.

"Oh," I said stupidly. "No, I'm... uh... I'm fine."

Perhaps the way my knees were trembling belied my words somewhat, but I was hoping this was just a matter of good old workout fatigue. While I'd made it a point to keep up with gentle yoga and Pilates routines even when I was struggling with my health, the truth was that this was the first serious physical workout I'd had in many years.

In a way, it kind of felt good to know that my muscles would be sore tomorrow. It made me feel like a normal person—ironic though that was under the current circumstances.

"As you like," Rans said, though his eyes on me were penetrating.

I wondered what he saw. Actually, no—scratch that. It was better if I didn't know. "I'll just… go get that drink from the kitchen," I mumbled, and fled the downstairs family room for the second time that afternoon.

The water was cool in my stomach, and the shower warm against my skin. After a few minutes of intense internal debate, I allowed myself an experiment. The tub-shower combo didn't have a detachable massaging showerhead, but I let my fingers play over my breasts and slide downward, teasing and rubbing my clit with the familiarity of long practice.

I tried not to think of Rans as I urged my body toward completion. Tried, and failed miserably. I bit my lip as the orgasm rolled through me, holding my breath to ensure that no sound would escape my lips. When the familiar buzz of endorphins eased, I leaned against the tub wall and took stock.

I felt… better, sort of. More relaxed, less shaky. Less stressed out. It didn't bring with it the sense of renewal that sex with another person—that sex with *Rans*—brought me. I didn't experience that feeling of being deliciously sated and rested, like I'd just eaten a gourmet meal and slept like a baby for eight solid hours.

It did help a little, but I knew full well that I couldn't sustain myself with masturbation in the long term. Hell, I'd already tried that approach, even if I hadn't known at the time that I was part succubus. It was clear that unless I wanted to end up as starved and debilitated as I'd been for much of the past several years, I would have to involve another person.

I would have to *feed* from another person. The thought left a bad taste in my mouth.

If I was serious about cutting Rans loose once I'd found Dad—if I was serious about protecting my dark angel from the raging dumpster fire that was my life now—how was I going to keep my strength up without him? Having sex with humans over the long term could hurt them… maybe even kill them.

Forget about my scruples, though—the plain truth was that something deep inside me howled in outrage at the idea of sleeping with another man. I tried to stomp on the little voice in hopes that it would shut up.

Come on… don't be stupid. We're talking about a centuries-old vampire here. Do you expect that he'll become celibate the moment you leave, and spend the rest of his immortal life pining for the American waitress who loved him and left him? As if!

It didn't help.

The prospect of spending the rest of my—probably abbreviated—life on the run from the Fae while engaging in random one-night hookups to stay alive was appalling beyond belief. In fact, the very idea made me shudder.

I wondered idly if I had to actually be involved in sexual activity to draw energy from it. Maybe I could become a professional voyeur, haunting raunchy sex clubs and paying desperate strippers to masturbate for me while I watched.

Ugh. Now I felt positively queasy.

Assuming I was strong enough to let Rans go before I dragged him down with me, the future was going to suck donkey balls. One thing was painfully clear, though. I was already becoming an addict. A vampire junkie. An undead groupie. A nosferatu…

Something.

It would be best if I kept my distance from Rans as much as humanly possible until we carried out whatever plan he and Albigard came up with, because I clearly couldn't be trusted around noble, attractive men with chronic iron deficiencies and sexy English accents.

I didn't see any way that my own faerie-tale was going to end well at this point. I wasn't sure if my dad's storyline could be salvaged or not, though I was bound and determined to try—no matter what the cost. But there was no reason Rans couldn't have a happy ending.

He just needed to avoid being dragged into my modern-day literary tragedy. And if Nigellus could eventually manage to talk him out of his self-destructive quest to poke the hornets' nest that was the war in hopes that answers would fly out, so much the better.

I finished showering and exited the bathroom with a towel wrapped around my body, rummaging through the small amount of clothing I owned for the least sexually suggestive options available, as a feeling of heaviness settled in my chest. T-shirt. Jeans. Done.

When I ventured forth, it was to the sound of Rans' muffled voice filtering through to me from the kitchen. I paused, but didn't hear any sign of a second person. Entering, I found him engaged in a phone conversation, and my excitement surged. He lifted a finger to forestall anything I might have been about to say, and pointed at the phone, mouthing, *Albigard*.

Eight

I bit my lip and perched on a chair, waiting. Rans' end of the conversation was unenlightening, and I chafed at not knowing what was being said. Finally, he ended the call and looked over at me.

"Well? What did he say?" I asked impatiently.

Rans turned to face me. "He was able to confirm that a high-level prisoner was transported to Dhuinne from this area. No details, but it seems fairly clear that it was your father."

My heart rate sped up. "We have to go after him," I said. "We have to sneak in somehow and—"

"*Zorah,*" he interrupted, "One does not *sneak into* Dhuinne."

I chewed the inside of my cheek. "There must be some way to get in!"

Rans sighed. "I told you that the entrance to the Fae realm lies inside a burial mound in County Meath, in Ireland. Perhaps I didn't make it clear that the entrance on the Hill of Tara is the *only* entrance. To say that it's well-guarded is putting it mildly."

I set my jaw and rose, pacing as I thought hard. "Then we'll have to… I don't know… make it so that they let us in voluntarily. Like, a Trojan Horse kind of thing, okay? I have to get in there,

Rans. I can't just leave Dad in their hands! Maybe if I pretended to be a prisoner—"

Hands closed on my upper arms, stopping my progress. I looked up, surprised. I hadn't even seen him move, I was so focused on brainstorming ways to get to my father.

"*Zorah.* Stop. You're not marching into the Fae realm like some kind of sacrificial offering."

I glared up at him.

"I'll speak with Nigellus," Rans continued, unperturbed by my scowl. "Possibly some other people, as well. Perhaps one of them can arrange some sort of diplomatic exchange with the Fae Court... some way to allow you contact with your father, and maybe get you off their hit list at the same time."

My lips were pressed together in a thin line. "And how likely is that?" I asked, my skepticism coming through clearly in my voice.

He didn't give ground, though. "I can't know until I try, now can I?" he shot back, a hint of frustration visible on his face. "But I do know this—you are *not* walking into Dhuinne without a guarantee of safe passage from someone with the power to back it up."

"Yeah? How long is all this likely to take, assuming it can be done at all?" I ground out.

"I'm not a fortune-teller, luv. Believe me, if I owned a functioning crystal ball, my life would be very different than what it is now." The words were uncompromising. "I'll call Nigellus next, and see what he has to say on the matter."

There was… something in his tone. Something that told me he didn't think the diplomatic option would work, and that if it didn't, he still wasn't going to budge on trying to get me into Dhuinne either openly or clandestinely.

My stomach churned, remembering what I'd said to him as I sat on the floor of my dad's ruined condo, holding the torn quilt that had belonged to my mother.

My only goal is to find my father. From this moment, that's the one thing I care about. As long as it's your goal, too, we're good. If I get a hint that it's not, then we have a serious problem.

I didn't want to end up in conflict with Rans. I really, really didn't.

"What if someone else went after Dad, instead of us?" I asked slowly. "Would Albigard do it? Could we… I don't know… bribe him? Or offer to do something for him in return?"

Rans' expression hardened. "There are areas in which I trust Albigard, and areas in which I don't. Sending him to deal with the Court face-to-face on your behalf falls firmly into the latter category."

I opened my mouth to say something angry—*great, so you're not willing to take me, but you won't let someone else go either*—but I stopped myself before the words could escape.

"Fine," I said. "Call Nigellus, then."

His expression was still set in a stony facade that covered a well of frustration. Rather than say anything, he thumbed through contacts and tapped one.

"Nigellus?" he said after a few moments. "I need your input on something. There's a bit of a... situation developing in Chicago."

I seethed quietly at having my determination to find and retrieve my father labeled a 'situation,' but I held my tongue as Rans concisely outlined what we'd discovered since arriving in the city.

"If one wanted to attempt travel into Dhuinne under prearranged diplomatic immunity, where would one start?" The words were tight enough to imply that the last thing Rans wanted was to get anyplace *near* Dhuinne, much less inside it.

He paused to let the voice on the other end reply, and a tendon in his jaw tightened. "Yes, I *know* it's bloody dangerous, Nigellus—I'm not mentally deficient!"

Another silence as Nigellus spoke.

"Bollocks. There must be someone who has a contact within the Court," Rans said. "You can't tell me no one has a backdoor line of communication at the ruling levels. If that were true, the damned treaty wouldn't have held for a decade, much less for more than two hundred years!"

The back and forth continued as I watched, chewing on a thumbnail. I couldn't make out anything of Nigellus' side, but Rans' side of the conversation grew more heated until he finally snapped, "The fucking treaty is in danger of breaking *now*! Goddamnit, Nigellus—" He broke off, and took in a deep breath, bringing his voice under control. "Just... think about it overnight. Let me know if there's anyone else who might have a different perspective on the matter."

Another pause, and Rans said, "Fine." Then he hung up.

I watched as he scrubbed a hand down his face. "He'll consider the options, and maybe try to talk to some people," he said, and I once again got that feeling of being *managed*.

"Great," I said flatly.

"I'll call a couple of other people I know," he said, his reply equally toneless. "Why don't you eat something and go get some rest. It's been… a day. I'll let you know if anything comes up. Otherwise, we can take a fresh look at things in the morning."

"Yeah, okay." I looked around the kitchen, my eyes falling on a fruit bowl. I grabbed a banana and an apple. "I guess I'm pretty tired after, well, everything."

It was hard, but I turned and walked out of the kitchen without a backward glance, returning to the room where I'd spent the previous night curled in Rans' arms. After a moment's thought, I gathered my things and moved them to another bedroom. It looked more lived-in, and I guessed it was Tom and Glynda's. Which… yes, was kind of a creepy thing for me to do. But I knew if Rans came in later and lay down next to me in bed, my determination not to get closer to him would crumple like a wet dishrag.

Moving to a different room was a pretty clear hands-off message, and one I was reasonably confident Mr. Middle Ages Chivalry would respect. I plonked my stuff down on the dresser and flopped onto the edge of the bed, eating my apple and banana. Then I lay back on the bed, still dressed, and thought things over.

Though it was early in the evening, I dozed a bit as the events of the day caught up with me. When I woke, it was fully dark outside, but I could hear the sounds of Rans moving around in the kitchen, along with the low murmur of his voice. He obviously hadn't been lying about talking to other people, which I appreciated.

It was still obvious that working out a diplomatic solution was a long shot, though. What was I going to do if no one could help? Leaving Dad in Fae hands for weeks while people who didn't really give a shit about him talked and debated endlessly was not an option. Hell, I'd already dicked around for days while who-knew-what was happening to him.

I felt a little sick at the thought of the hours I'd spent having sex with Rans... training with Rans... sleeping curled in Rans' arms. All of this, while my father was a prisoner.

At least, you hope *he's a prisoner,* said my unhelpful internal voice.

I shoved my doubts into the dark place reserved for things I didn't want to examine too closely. The point was, the Fae could be doing anything to Darryl Bright right now, and I was lying here on a comfortable bed in a safe house, napping after my pleasant shower.

What the hell kind of daughter was I? It was one thing to be unable to act yet. It was totally another to spend time relaxing and having a good time while my father was in the hands of my enemies.

In the morning, I resolved, I would take action with or without Rans and his diplomatic solution. The point that everyone seemed to be forgetting—myself included—was that I was basically fucked no matter what happened. The Fae wanted me gone. The demons probably wished I didn't exist in the first place, since my existence put the treaty at risk. I could count the number of humans who would be upset by my disappearance on one hand.

The only person who seemed committed to protecting me was a single, slightly unhinged vampire… who also happened to be the person I cared most about protecting. Rans was the most likely person to end up as collateral damage in the Fae's witch-hunt against me, and he was one of the two people in my life right now who I would die to protect.

The realization struck me in the chest like a blow.

And yet, the more I rolled it around in my mind, the more true it felt. I would die to protect my father because he was my family, and because I hadn't been in a position to protect my mother in her time of need. But I would die to protect Rans because it seemed increasingly likely that I wasn't going to survive being hunted by the Fae, and saving the man who had tried to save me would give my death some kind of meaning.

I'd been moments from being whisked away by Caspian at the bus station in St. Louis. Alma's knife blade had missed slamming through my eye and into my brain by mere inches, and the Fae hadn't even known I was in Chicago at the time. My life hung by the barest of threads these days.

Much of my life had been spent as a victim, and a fairly pathetic one at that. I'd been a victim of the gunman who'd taken my mother's life when I was six. A victim of my father's emotional distance and neglect. A victim of my chronic health problems, both physical and mental. Was it such an unreasonable desire to want to make one final, grand gesture before the Fae snuffed out my existence?

If I failed, at least it would be on my terms. And besides, once they had me, why would the Fae need to keep my father anyway? They might make my skin crawl, but it was obvious the Fae were a civilized society in many ways. If they granted last requests, I would make mine my father's freedom. Or, at the very least, his safety.

And then it would all be over. Dad could congratulate himself on having been right all along about my coming to a bad end. Rans would be safer, and maybe Nigellus could convince him to back off in his quest to find out the details of how he had survived the war.

While I… I would be gone. I wouldn't have to run anymore. I wouldn't have to feel this constant sensation of dread over what horrible thing was going to happen next in my life. I wouldn't have to fight against my stupid emotions… my misplaced and pathetic feelings for someone who couldn't possibly care for me the way I wanted him to.

I would give Rans the night to come up with a better plan, just as I'd agreed—even though I knew with utter certainty that all of his efforts would be in vain. And in the morning? Well... I now knew exactly what I needed to do to fix all of this.

I didn't sleep again that night. As the hours passed, I listened to Rans' voice filtering through to me intermittently, barely audible through the walls. I had to give credit where credit was due; he obviously hadn't been putting me off with his promises to talk to anyone who might be able to help.

As the night wore on, though, the silences grew longer and the conversations shorter. He was running out of options, running out of ideas. As I'd known they would, all his efforts had come to nothing.

Some childish impulse had me pretending to sleep when his footsteps approached along the hall. I heard him pause outside of the bedroom we'd shared the previous night, standing still and silent for a long moment as though contemplating the empty bed. Then his tread approached the closed door of the master bedroom. Another pause, and he knocked lightly on the door before opening it.

The clock on the bedside table read a quarter to five in glowing red numbers.

"Zorah, wake up."

I made a production of blinking awake and sitting upright, still not sure why I felt the need to act like I'd been sleeping. "Yeah?"

"I just wanted to update you." His normally smooth voice sounded tired and a bit raspy from all the phone conversations. "No joy yet, but we'll try again later in the morning. I'm... going to have a kip for a couple of hours, so I can take a fresh look at things after I've had some rest."

I hesitated for a beat. "Okay."

He remained motionless in the doorway for the space of several breaths before he stepped back, closing the door behind him with a soft click. His footsteps receded, heading for the guest bedroom before the sound faded, muted by the carpet.

I lay in Tom and Glynda's bed, not moving, trying to decipher the small sounds coming from down the hall. I watched the clock, my mind a careful blank as the numbers changed in slow motion.

Dawn's not a great time for vampires.

The words echoed in my memory as five o'clock rolled around... five-fifteen... five-thirty. As six a.m. approached, the house had been silent for some time. I carefully got out of bed. Dawn's gray light was just beginning to illuminate the unfamiliar room. I snuck over to the dresser where I'd dumped my meager belongings and pulled on a pair of sneakers. Then I retrieved one of my burner phones from my bag, moving as silently as I could manage.

Phone in hand, I eased the bedroom door open an inch at a time. It hadn't creaked when Rans had opened and closed it earlier, but I didn't need any shrill squeaks giving me away. Tiptoeing along the hallway, I paused at the open door of the guest bedroom and looked inside. Rans was asleep on top of the duvet, his body displaying that same disconcerting stillness I'd noticed the previous morning.

I'd only intended to ensure that he wasn't awake, but I ended up standing there for far longer than I should have, watching him. He'd understand why I had to do this, I thought. He'd know I was only acting to minimize the damage to those around me.

Wouldn't he?

My heart was thumping against my chest as I looked at those finely sculpted features barely illuminated by the dawn light. It was that powerful thud-thud-thud against the cage of my ribs that finally unglued my feet and got me moving again. I was afraid he might be able to hear it. To sense the thrum of blood through my veins.

After a final lingering look, I crept downstairs and carefully unlocked the sliding door leading to the back yard. I winced a bit at the sound of the door sliding along the track, but I was committed at this point. I went outside into the muggy Chicago morning, the phone clutched in my hand.

The back yard was on the opposite side of the house from the guest bedroom, but I still moved as far away from the house as I could get. The fence around the yard was a bit of a hodgepodge—chain link on two sides and wooden privacy fence on the other two. I wedged myself in the corner of the privacy fence and powered up the phone.

Pulling up the contacts, I scrolled through the numbers I'd copied from Rans' phone yesterday when I'd been waiting for him in the car, and selected the entry labeled 'Tink.' The cheap phone displayed a graphic of a bell ringing as the call connected. I held my breath, not sure in the least that the recipient of my early-morning call would even bother to pick up.

The line crackled, but the other end remained silent.

"Hello?" I asked, tentative. "Albigard?"

Another pause, just long enough to make me think I'd made a mistake. Then…

"Hello, demonkin." Albigard's voice made it sound like there were many other things he would rather be doing than speaking to me. *"I had wondered if you might contact me today."*

Nine

"You... did?" I asked. "Why? And how did you know it was me?" I'd expected to have to explain myself—how I got this number, why I was calling.

"Your father has been transported to Dhuinne. No doubt the bloodsucker has been scrambling for a way to convince you not to do something foolish to try and get him back, even though he knows there is no safe way for you to reach him."

The truth of those words burned. "Something like that," I muttered.

"Did you wait until he fell asleep to sneak out and speak to me?" Now the barest hint of amusement colored the Fae's tone.

"Yes," I told him, "I sure did. So, what can you do for me?"

"Do for you? In what capacity, demonkin?"

"Don't play dumb. Can you get me into to Dhuinne? Can you get me to my father?"

Albigard sighed. *"Yes, and very possibly. But those are not the questions you should be asking."*

I steeled myself, because I already suspected what the answer to my third question would be. So I asked a different one. "Can you get my father out of there, once they have me as a prisoner instead?"

There was a rather long pause.

"Well?" I pressed.

"That... was not precisely the question I expected."

"That's nice," I snapped. "So what's the answer?"

"The answer is... perhaps." Albigard paused again. "If your intention is truly to give yourself over to the Fae Court, it may be possible to negotiate your father's release in exchange."

"Okay, great." I stood up, pacing next to the tall wooden fence in an attempt to release some of the nervous jitters building inside me. "When can we leave? I'll have to sneak out and call a cab or something so I can meet you, but I should leave before Rans wakes up and—"

I stumbled to a halt, my words trailing off as a burning oval appeared in the air in front of me. Albigard stepped through, and the portal collapsed in on itself, disappearing. He looked... wilder and less civilized than I remembered, clad in loose pants and a soft shirt that exposed the dark web of tattoos climbing up his collarbones to stretch toward the base of his throat. His feet were bare in the brown-tipped summer grass of the suburban back yard.

"Uh..." I began, staring.

His sharp brows drew together. "Come. I am about to make an enemy out of an ally. I would prefer to gain some tangible benefit from the move before the inevitable battle ensues."

"How did you know where I was?" I blurted.

His tone grew dry, and his expression sour. "You drank my mead, demonkin. You also tried to drink *me*."

"And that means you can track me down now, just like that?" I asked in disbelief.

He gestured around us, as if to say, *well, obviously*. I dragged my thoughts back to the practical. Did it really matter, given what I was about to do? Pretty soon, every Fae in existence would know *exactly* where I was. I had to fight a shudder at the idea, my resolve wavering for the first time.

I shoved my fear down and away. *Don't think about it. Just act. Think of Dad.*

"Fine. When can we go?" The longer I had to wait, the less I trusted myself not to have second thoughts.

Rather than answer in words, Albigard swept his hand in a circle through the air, and a new portal opened in front of us. He gestured me through, and I forced heavy feet to step forward. To step *through*.

I held my breath through the disorientation, unsure if I'd be stepping out into Dhuinne, or the basement cells in Albigard's house, or what. It turned out to be none of those things. Instead, Albigard emerged to stand next to me in what must have once been a parking lot, before nature made a spirited attempt to reclaim it.

Ahead, a large, square-cornered institutional building lay in ruins. It appeared to be from the 1940s or 50s. The windows were long gone, leaving dark, gaping eyes in the structure. Rusty, acid-rain streaks ran down the exterior walls.

"What is this place?" I whispered, my voice feeling intrusive in the early morning silence.

The portal closed behind us with a wave of Albigard's hand. "Abandoned hospital. It's positioned on the ley line that leads to the Hill of Tara."

A small shiver ran up the length of my spine. "Is this where my father was transported from?"

"No. That was further west of here."

I remembered the series of dots on Derrick's map, and wondered if the *Weekly Oracle* crew had EMF detection equipment hidden somewhere on the premises. Certainly, the place looked like vacation paradise for ghost hunters.

Albigard was already striding toward the front entrance of the derelict building, and I scrambled to follow him. "So," I asked, catching up, "how does this work? Another portal, this time all the way to Ireland?"

I'd never been out of the country before, I realized with a small pang. Never even left the small, bi-state area comprised of Missouri and Illinois until Rans had jetted me to Atlantic City a few days ago…

No. Don't think of Rans right now.

Albigard threw me a dark, side-eyed look. "Not exactly."

He strode deeper into the decaying building, as though following an invisible trail. Then we were descending a questionable looking staircase, and—seriously, what the hell was it with Fae and basements? But the answer became clear a moment later, when we approached a patch of dusty light, the beam filtering in from a high, narrow window in the outer wall. It illuminated an area where the concrete floor had been dug up in chunks, revealing bare, dark earth beneath. I thought I could see worms and pill bugs crawling around in the damp dirt.

"A moment," Albigard said, before closing his eyes and murmuring in that unfamiliar language he sometimes used. He gestured down the length of his own body. The loose sleep clothing he'd been wearing dissolved, replaced by soft buckskin boots that laced to the knee, fitted breeches in a shade of dark forest green, a shirt of unbleached linen in a loose weave, half-unlaced at the throat, and a buckskin vest. His loose, blond hair wove itself into intricate braids as I watched, open-mouthed.

"Okay," I managed. "That's... handy."

Damn. I hadn't been too far off with my Legolas comments when we'd first met. His presence still grated against my nerves, but it was clear that for the first time, I was seeing Albigard as he was meant to be seen—not as his kind tried to present themselves to fit in on Earth.

"Come." He took me by the upper arm, ignoring the way I stiffened, and pulled me to stand on the exposed dirt.

I clamped my jaw against my need for him *not to be touching me,* knowing he didn't mean anything untoward by the gesture. Indeed, once I was where he wanted me, he let go as if he were no more pleased by the contact than I was.

He crouched next to me, placing one palm flat on the damp earth. A faint glow spread outward from the contact until it surrounded both of us. With a few murmured words, our surroundings faded out, leaving blackness shot through with streaks of color that hurt my eyes until I closed them.

It was like stepping through one of his portals, but... worse. Or rather, it was *more,* somehow. I wasn't really falling, but I felt like I should be. I desperately wanted something to hang onto, but there was nothing, and I refused to grab for Albigard's arm like a frightened child. The sensation of blinding movement lasted way, *way* too long. But then I was... elsewhere... staggering in surroundings even more dimly lit than the hospital basement had been.

"Where—?" I gasped, catching one hand against a damp stone wall.

Evidently our tentative agreement hadn't given Albigard any more patience with me than he'd had before, because he only growled, "Where do you think?" and led the way deeper into the darkened tunnel.

I tried to remember what Rans had said about the gateway between Earth and Dhuinne. It was in County Meath, on the Hill of Tara, in the Mound of... something or the other?

So, this was Ireland, then. Apparently. It was too bad I wouldn't get a chance to see other parts of it that were less... *underground.* I tried to focus on my surroundings, because the alternative was to focus on how close I was to the point of no return with a plan that would most likely end in my death.

Albigard stopped in front of what appeared to be a dead end. The light filtering through from the tunnel entrance behind us barely illuminated primitive symbols marked on the wall. I saw spirals and simple line drawings, the whole thing giving me a vaguely Celtic vibe.

I swallowed against the dryness in my throat, trying hard not to think of Rans and how he would react when he woke to find me gone.

"What will the Fae do to me?" I asked. "I mean, exactly? Do you know?"

"I've no idea," he said, placing a hand on the central symbol. "These days the Court can barely come to agreement on the simplest issues. No doubt the Unseelie wish you dead, while the Seelie may well prefer to study you first in hopes of determining how you came to be."

I clenched my fists to hold in a shudder. "How do they execute people in Dhuinne?"

Albigard shrugged. "Beheading, generally. It is quick and relatively painless when performed skillfully." He paused in whatever he was doing to glance down at me, his green eyes luminous in the low light. "I must say, your decision to pursue this course surprises me, demonkin."

I tried to ignore the way my heart was pounding like a drum. "Yeah? It shouldn't. I'm not a fool. Your people are going to catch up to me sooner or later. Probably sooner. This way, Rans won't be standing in front of me when it happens, and I have a chance of helping my father. It's only logical."

"That is the part which surprises me," Albigard said, still studying me like I was a bug who'd stood up on its hind legs and started doing calculus.

I glowered at him. "Could you maybe not insult me when I'm preparing to go to my doom?"

He flickered an eyebrow and returned his attention to the symbols. "My apologies." A glow began to spread out from his hand where it pressed against the wall, similar to what had happened at the old hospital. "In case it isn't clear," he continued, "as soon as the gate opens, you will be my prisoner. I will take you to wherever your father is being kept, unless someone with more authority stops me. At some point, you will be taken away from me, but you have my word that I will attempt to leverage your capture to gain your father's release."

"And how much authority do you have, exactly?" I couldn't keep the wariness from my tone.

Green eyes flashed at me. "That, unfortunately, is a very complicated question these days."

I nodded, trying not to think about Rans' words earlier.

There are areas in which I trust Albigard, and areas in which I don't. Sending him to deal with the Court face-to-face on your behalf falls firmly into the latter category.

"What's in this for you?" I asked.

"Renewed standing with the Court," he said without hesitation. "Access to people who may be of use to me in the future."

"And that's worth making an enemy of Rans?"

I was stalling now, and I knew it. But I'd still feel more confident going into this if I could get a better understanding of Albigard's motives up front.

He paused for the barest of moments. "That remains to be seen. It is… a calculated risk, given current events. We are embroiled in a dynamic situation, in which unexpected developments require immediate responses." He shot me a final look. "You are correct, though, that the Fae would have found you in fairly short order. And, from what little I have seen, you are also correct about the vampire's likely actions in the face of your imminent capture."

"I just want to minimize the collateral damage as much as I can," I said quietly. "There aren't many people in this world I give a damn about. I don't want those people hurt because of me. Not if I can help it."

"There is honor in that, demonkin," Albigard said.

The glow was spreading across the entire wall now, becoming bright enough to hurt my eyes. I blinked rapidly, trying to see through the sheen of tears that had formed across my vision. What lay on the other side of the wall was… not Earth. Panic tried to rise, tried to pull my feet away from the vision of elsewhere.

I was looking at Dhuinne, the place that had spawned these beings whose presence I could barely stand. I was giving myself over to them. Placing myself in the hands of creatures like Caspian Werther. Once I stepped into that world, it was very likely that I would never see this one again.

I stumbled back a single step before I caught myself.

Stop.

Dad's freedom.

Rans' safety.

Have you ever played that stupid hypothetical game where you try to decide if you would sacrifice yourself for your loved ones in a crisis? Almost everyone convinces themselves that they would be a hero during an emergency… but when the rubber hits the road, most people don't run into the burning building. They don't jump in front of the active shooter, or dive into the freezing water to save the drowning victim.

They save themselves instead.

There was an important difference in this case, though. It seemed highly unlikely that I would be able to save myself. Even trying to do so would mean a life on the run, always looking over my shoulder, wondering every time I faced a new person if they would scream 'Demon!' and pull a weapon before trying to kill me.

Rans thought he could put an iron dagger in my hand and teach me to fight the monsters, but I wasn't at all sure I could live that life. I wasn't sure I wanted to become that person. I *did* want Rans to be safe. I wanted my dad to be safe.

I stepped forward again.

Albigard's hand closed around my upper arm, and I tried not to tremble.

"Come, Zorah Bright," he said. "Your father is waiting in Dhuinne."

He pulled me through the space where the wall had been. It was much worse than traveling by portal or ley line, and I nearly doubled over as my stomach tried to rebel at the strangeness of traveling between realms. Albigard hauled me upright, stumbling, and through swimming vision I saw a phalanx of guards blocking our way with swords, crossbows, and glowing balls of magic in their hands.

"State your purpose, Wing Commander," said the guard at the front. "Why do you bring this creature into Dhuinne unannounced?"

With a jolt, I took in the features of the guards surrounding us. They weren't *human*. Which seemed a ridiculous thing to realize when I'd just traveled to a different planet—but all the Fae I'd seen to this point had appeared human enough. I glanced at Albigard, unable to hold back a gasp at the sight of his face in profile.

His hair remained the intricately braided mass of spun gold it had been on Earth, but those braids now exposed faun-like ears swept to a delicate point, along with dark eyebrows that would have made Mr. Spock from Star Trek jealous. His skin seemed to glow with some inner iridescence. It made him almost hard for me to look at.

He stared down his nose at the guard who had challenged him.

"I have a second prisoner from the Chicago overkeep," he said in a cold, haughty voice. "She is to be placed with the other one that was brought in recently. The human. Where was that one taken?"

The guard hesitated, as though Albigard had gone off-script somehow. I tried not to succumb to panic as the proximity of so many armed Fae made my instincts scream with the need to flee. Albigard only continued to stare down the guards like they were dirt on his boot.

Eventually, the guard's resistance crumbled, and he broke eye contact with my erstwhile captor. "The human was taken to the eastern quarter, and handed over to the Recorder's office."

Albigard's fingers tightened on my arm—a convulsive twitch so brief I wasn't quite sure I'd truly felt it—but nothing came through in his voice as he issued a curt, "Very well," and strode forward, dragging me behind him.

I held my breath as we approached the line of stony, inhuman faces, but at the last moment the phalanx of guards parted. Albigard passed through them like Moses at the parting of the Red Sea, with me still held firmly in tow.

"I will inform the Court of your arrival, *Commander Albigard,*" the guard threw after us, and I was sure I hadn't imagined the sting behind those words.

But Albigard only waved the statement off carelessly with his free hand. "Yes. Do so." The retort sounded positively bored.

Ten

I tried to take everything in as I was dragged away. There were buildings here—functional and laid out around the place where we'd appeared in such a way as to make me think it was a military encampment. That would certainly make sense, if this was really the only way into Dhuinne from Earth. It was also clear that Rans had been right—sneaking into Dhuinne had been a total pipe dream.

It wasn't the buildings and soldiers that held my attention, however; it was the world itself. Dhuinne was bursting with life. Or at least, this part of it was. Vines and flowers covered everything the Fae had built here. Trees arched over the buildings, grass tried to choke out the cobblestone walkways beneath our feet, huge leaves clustered at the base of every fence and lamppost. I could almost swear that when I stared at the rampant plant life for long enough, I could actually see it moving and growing.

Above me, pink and white clouds sculled across a lavender sky. Rather than a yellow cast, the light from the sun was an actinic white. And… it was way up in the sky, too. When we'd left Chicago, it had been just past sunrise.

Of course, then we'd gone to Ireland, which was several time zones ahead—

I shook my head, trying to dislodge the meaningless musing over trivia before it gave me a headache. At the edge of the town, or outpost, or whatever it was, Albigard came to a halt and called up a portal.

I didn't dare ask where we were going or what was likely to happen once we got there—not while I was playing the cowed prisoner. Though perhaps calling what I was doing an act was something of a polite fiction at this point. I was a prisoner, and I was pretty fucking cowed right now.

Albigard hauled me through the portal and closed it behind us. The military outpost had given the impression of being a small settlement in a rural area, but now we were in an honest-to-god city. Weirdly, it was still choked with plant life in a way Earth cities weren't—at least, not unless they'd been abandoned and left to rot for years.

Yet for all the aggressive, jungle-like fauna, there was no sense of decay. No smell of rotting leaves or mold; no buildup of dead plants piling up on the ground. Everything was just… *alive.*

We had arrived in what appeared to be some sort of courtyard behind an impressive structure. The building was surrounded by many other impressive structures, making me wonder if this was some sort of government district where the so-called Recorder's office could be found. Except for the rampant wildlife, it reminded me of the older parts of St. Louis with their ornate churches and two-hundred-year-old courthouses.

There were more Fae here, bustling about in the way of people everywhere who had places to be and important things to do. Albigard marched me into the building, and I was a bit shocked that the riot of plant life even existed inside the grand old structure. Vines choked the banisters of staircases and dripped from the ceiling in sprays of flowers. Their heavy perfume filled the air.

It was beautiful… and it made me want to run away in the same way that the Fae themselves made me want to run away. But I couldn't run away. Where would I run? For all I knew, we could be miles away from the gate where we had come in. The gate that was guarded by dozens of magic-wielding warriors who could kill me with a single blow.

I had made my decision, and now there would be no turning back.

We approached an alcove full of shelves, getting surprised and wary looks from those we passed. What I had briefly taken to be carpet under my feet turned out to be moss in a much bluer shade of green than anything I'd ever seen growing on Earth.

An immensely old Fae poked his head out from between two sets of shelves. Rather than books, they held scrolls. Albigard strode up to the elderly man, ignoring the disconcerted mutters in our wake. I tried to look meek and non-threatening while still sneaking occasional peeks at my surroundings.

Christ. Even this white-haired, stoop-shouldered old guy set off my creepy-crawliness.

Did all demons react this way to all Fae? If so, no wonder they'd ended up at war. It was clear that this ancient dude was some kind of paper-pusher—no threat to anyone. It made me worry about how I'd react when the ones who really *were* a threat showed up. I wondered when that would be.

I didn't want my last acts to consist of screaming and thrashing and begging for mercy, but I guess in the end, the details of my final moments didn't matter to anyone but me. The most important part was making it to Dad before the truly bad stuff started happening. It would be Albigard who arranged for his release, if all went well—and please, god, let me not have made a mistake in trusting him on that—but I desperately wanted to see my father one last time.

I wanted to see with my own eyes that he was a prisoner and not a collaborator. I wanted to tell him that I was sorry for making him so miserable, for putting him in danger, and that I loved him. I wanted to say goodbye.

"Recorder," Albigard was saying, "I need information on the whereabouts of a human prisoner brought into Dhuinne two days ago."

The old man scowled, first at Albigard and then at me. "And you are...?"

Albigard waved the fingers of his free hand and a sigil crackled in the air before him. It was made of the same fiery *whatever* as the portals he created, but it was much smaller and shot through with a complex pattern that reminded me of the tattoos at the base of his throat.

"Oh." The Recorder's scowl faded, but his expression still looked sour. "You're *that* one."

"*The prisoner*?" Albigard prompted, sounding like he didn't want to be having this conversation any more than Old Guy apparently did.

"An unusual case," Old Guy said grudgingly, eyeing me with clear distaste. "He was registered as a prisoner, true—but he had previously been recorded as a cull."

He might as well have been speaking Greek for all I was able to glean from that statement, but Albigard's eyebrows shot up.

"Is that so?" he asked mildly, and the old man shrugged.

"He was taken to the former owner's dwelling," the Recorder said in a tone that made it obvious he didn't approve.

"And the address?" Albigard pressed.

The Recorder's rheumy eyes narrowed. "Why do you need it?"

"Because this prisoner is to be delivered to the same place."

I held my breath. The Recorder continued to stare Albigard down for long moments, but then a canny look crossed his wrinkled face.

"As you like, Commander. I'll retrieve it for you now. I assume you'll be going straight there?"

Albigard merely continued to look at him, expressionless. A smile twitched on the old man's face, and he excused himself to the stacks, returning a few moments later with a page that looked like real parchment. Albigard glanced at it, and turned away without another word to the Recorder.

"Come," he said, tugging me after him.

I let myself be hurried along, back down the vine-choked stairwell, through the perfumed atrium dripping with blossoms, and outside.

"Did you get the address?" I asked.

"Quiet," he said. Then, in a lower voice, "The residence is some distance from here, and the Recorder will almost certainly inform the city guard to meet us there."

"Can't you magic us to wherever this place is?" I muttered, ignoring his command for silence.

"I have never been there before, so—no."

"You'd never been to the house where I was staying in Chicago, either!" I hissed.

"I used your presence there as my anchor," he replied in a tone that made it clear I should shut up now. "Move your feet, demonkin, unless you want to find the guards waiting for us when we arrive."

I gritted my teeth and half-jogged to keep up with his long strides. This place would have been fascinating under any other circumstances. The surroundings were just similar enough to my own world that most things were identifiable, yet everything was slightly *off*, like the blue-green moss carpet. Like the too-perfect glamoured appearance the Fae used on Earth.

There were people around, but it wasn't crowded in the way downtown St. Louis or Chicago were crowded during the daylight hours. Statuesque men and lovely, elfin-featured women gave us looks that ranged from disdainful to worried as Albigard dragged me along at speed.

Gradually, the tenor of our surroundings changed from *this-is-where-people-work* to *this-is-where-people-live*. The roads grew narrower, or at least the usable portion that hadn't been taken over by plant life grew narrower. The buildings grew smaller, the layout of streets less regular.

Albigard glanced up at each intersection, and I noticed signs, covered in symbols I couldn't decipher. Which, now that I thought about it, raised a rather obvious question.

"We're almost there," Albigard said, turning right onto an even narrower street.

"How can I understand the language here?" I blurted. "I certainly can't read the writing."

He shot me a dark, sidelong glance. "How many times do I have to remind you that you drank my mead? I'm translating for you, obviously. You're welcome, by the way."

And, okay—I wasn't going to examine that response too closely. If Albigard was creepy-crawling around inside my head somehow, I was happier not knowing the details. Even so, I shivered involuntarily.

"Er, yeah. Thanks," I managed.

Our pace hadn't slackened during the exchange, and now Albigard gestured to a cute little cottage that looked pretty much like all the other cute little cottages on this stretch of road.

"Here," he said as we turned onto the stone-lined walkway leading to the front door. "It appears the guards haven't arrived yet."

He knocked briskly on the weathered wood. For a long moment, nothing happened, but then I heard the click of a lock disengaging and the door creaked inward. No one was standing inside to greet us, though I thought I caught sight of something small and dark darting out of the front room. An animal, maybe?

Albigard's brow furrowed. He gave the interior a slow look, as though searching out possible traps.

"Is this it?" I asked nervously. "Is he here?"

"Allegedly," he said, which wasn't nearly as reassuring a response as it might have been.

He let go of my arm, and I shook it out as the blood flow returned. I pushed past him into the house, figuring that at this point, there wasn't much worse that could happen to me than what was already going to happen. Time wasn't exactly on my side, so caution could go take a flying leap.

"Hello?" I called.

Nobody answered.

The place was small, so I headed deeper into the cottage, aware of Albigard trailing after me. Again, I noted the sort of sideways familiarity of the structure. I was able to identify the kitchen, though I would have struggled to use it to prepare food. The table and chairs in the dining area were recognizable enough, as was the collection of comfortable seating arranged around a fireplace in what was clearly the living area.

Something seemed off, though, and it took me longer than it should have to realize that it was the relative lack of invading plant life inside the place.

Aside from a few herbs trying to overflow their pots on various windowsills, there were no choking vines or heavy-scented flowers here. No moss growing on the floor—just neatly swept hardwood planks covered in places by homey woven rugs.

Movement caught my eye—a dark tail flicking as whatever it was attached to ducked through the doorway on the far side of the living area. I followed it, glancing back to find Albigard settling himself next to a front-facing window and twitching the curtain back.

Keeping watch, I realized.

I didn't have long. The door through which the dark tail had disappeared was half open.

"Hello?" I asked, more tentatively this time.

Still no answer, but I thought I heard a faint rustling noise coming from within. The hinges creaked as I opened the door further. Inside was a bedroom, and I had a vague sense of light fabrics and airy, pleasant surroundings before my eyes lit on a figure seated on a rocking chair in one corner, facing half away from me.

My hand slipped from the knob, dropping limply to my side.

"Dad?" I asked in a small voice, my heart leaping into my throat and trying to choke me.

My father didn't move or acknowledge my presence in any way, and a chill slid across my skin despite the pleasant warmth of the air.

On the bed, a huge black cat with slanted green eyes that seemed too large for its face regarded me. An odd rumble of sound emerged from its throat, and then it lifted one front paw to its muzzle, tongue swiping out to groom itself as though my presence here was of no further interest to it one way or the other.

Swallowing hard, I forced my feet to carry me into the room until I was standing directly in front of my father's chair. He didn't move, the chair resting motionless on its curved wooden rockers. His eyes were focused on nothing, staring right through me. I shivered.

Please, please, please let me not have come all this way only to find that Darryl Bright was gone, only the empty shell of a body left behind, I thought. *Please let me not be too late.*

Albigard entered, throwing the cat a disgusted look when it growled low in its chest at him. "Guards are approaching. They will be here momentarily, at which point you will once again be my prisoner."

"What's wrong with him?" I begged.

The Fae ran careless eyes over the man in the chair. "He's broken, apparently. It happens sometimes, with humans." He paused for the barest instant before adding, "I am sorry, demonkin."

I made a small noise in my throat and dropped to my knees, my hands gripping Dad's where they rested on the chair's arms. "Dad, *please...*"

My father's eyes focused slowly, returning from that distant, unseen place. I caught my breath.

"Dad?"

He blinked, looking at me properly for the first time, and his brow furrowed. "Zorah? Why are you here? I don't want you here. Go away."

His voice was perfectly flat, and I had to swallow a moan of denial. Before I could respond, the front door crashed open. The cat hissed again, leaping from its perch on the bed as several Fae appeared at the bedroom's entrance. Albigard dragged me to my feet and swung us around, cool and collected as though armed guards swarmed the room where he was standing every day of the week.

"Hold, Sergeant," he said, sounding arrogant and bored. Disdain dripped from his voice. "I have an important prisoner for the Court to examine."

The guard looked at me like one might look at a wounded mouse caught in a mousetrap.

"Commander," he said grudgingly. "This is the part-bred demon? If it's your prisoner, why bring it here?"

I might have appreciated the jaundiced look Albigard gave the guard if my heart weren't trying to thud its way straight out of my chest.

"That one is her sire," he said, jerking his chin toward the rocking chair. "Where else would I deliver her? You and your men are here now, are you not? So take her off my hands and be done with it."

The guard wavered. "Very well," he said eventually. "But I will give a full accounting of all this to the Recorder."

Albigard cocked a slanted brow. "As you like, Sergeant. Though, as the Recorder was the one who directed me here, it seems rather a waste of time and effort."

With that, he handed me over to the wiry Sergeant, who regarded me with distaste. When the

Fae guard's hand closed around my arm, I felt my future narrow to a single point of darkness.

"I love you, Dad," I croaked… but my father had already returned to whatever distant place he now inhabited. A place I could no longer reach. He didn't even look at me as I was pulled from the room.

"Come, part-breed," the sergeant grumbled, tugging me away from my only tie to Earth… to my home.

Eleven

I threw a final glance over my shoulder at Albigard, trying to convey the threat of dire consequences if he failed to do all he could for whatever was left of my father. He gazed back with every indication of complete disinterest, his green eyes without expression.

I had played the only card available to me, bet everything on this gamble. And there was every possibility that doing so had gained me precisely nothing. Nothing except a faster death than I might've had before, assuming the Fae decided to take the easy way out and have done with me.

At least Rans is safe, I tried to tell myself. With me gone, they would have no reason to go after him.

Yeah, sure, said the little internal voice that whispered bad things to me in the dark. *Just like no one had a reason to blast a hole through his chest with a shotgun. He hadn't even met you yet when that happened.*

My throat tightened, denial burning like acid at the backs of my eyes. Jesus, I was such an idiot.

That's the real reason he's better off without you, the voice whispered. *Your own dad doesn't even want you. Nobody wants you. Hell, you can probably count the number of people who'll even notice that you're gone on the fingers of one hand.*

I wrenched my attention outward, consigning that little voice to the darkness where it belonged.

"Where are you taking me?" I asked my captors, the words emerging unsteady.

The guards—half a dozen or so—formed a loose ring around us as the sergeant frog-marched me out of the little cottage. No one answered or even acknowledged that I'd spoken. The one at the front paused and muttered, throwing a new portal into existence. It seemed less stable than the ones I'd seen Albigard make—the outline hazy and wavering—but the others didn't hesitate to step through.

A moment of sickening disorientation, and I was once more in the overgrown, downtowny looking area that Albigard and I had departed from earlier. Indeed, we were outside the very same building, I was fairly sure, though this time the sergeant hauled me around to a back entrance rather than walking in the front door.

The same white-haired Recorder guy met us, satisfaction visible on his wrinkled features. "So, you found the malcontent waiting there as I thought you would. Very good."

"Yes, sir," said the sergeant. "Shall I take this creature to the incarceration area now?"

"Do so," said the Recorder. "I will make the necessary entry into the records. And I believe there is at least one operative on Earth who will appreciate being notified of its capture."

That would probably sound ominous, if anything that happened to me now could be said to be more ominous than anything else. I was dragged back outside—making me wonder if it was considered impolite to open a portal inside a building or something. Maybe there were official portal zones that you had to use?

Whatever the case, Shaky Portal-Making Guy threw a new one up in the courtyard behind the Recorder's building. A moment later, he and my captor took me through it. When we stepped out, I staggered a bit, looking around in surprise. Silly me, I'd assumed the incarceration area would be some variant on Albigard's creepy basement cells.

Wow, had I been wrong.

We were in… something that looked an awful lot like the inside of a giant redwood tree that had been hollowed out, as crazy as that sounded. The area was more or less circular, maybe seven or eight feet in diameter, and surrounded by rough walls. Only they weren't really *walls,* as such. It was simply a hollow tree trunk made of unfinished, unaltered, living wood with no doors, windows, or other openings. The floor was packed dirt with twisted tree roots poking up through the surface here and there. There was a small hole dug near the edge, and the hole stank so badly of stale urine and feces that I nearly gagged.

I whirled around, taking it all in, and claustrophobia prickled at the edges of my mind. Then I craned my head up, trying to see where the light was coming from, and immediately grew dizzy. The walls… the *tree*… rose far above my head.

Like, *dozens of feet* above my head, at a minimum. It looked completely unclimbable, with no hand or footholds that I could see. The illumination filtering in from the top appeared to be natural daylight.

"No," I said a bit desperately as the reality of what was happening set in. "Please… don't leave me in here."

The guard who had been holding onto me gave me a shove, sending me crashing against the unforgiving wood of what was to become my living prison. He and Shaky Portal-Making Guy stepped back through the hazy ring hovering in the air. I pushed away from the wall and tried to lunge after them, but the portal snapped shut before I could reach it. All I succeeded in doing was staggering to a halt against the other side of the tree.

"*Shit!*" I yelled. The sound echoed hollowly around me.

I tried to quiet my uneven breathing. I was okay. No one had hurt me, unless you counted the bruise where my shoulder had hit the inside of the tree. I needed to slow down and assess things without panicking.

The hole in the floor was meant as a primitive latrine, judging by the stench. A pile of objects lay on the floor, directly across from the shit pit. I'd barely noticed them sitting there during my brief flirtation with hysteria. I approached the pile and crouched, examining the items in the uncertain light filtering down from above.

There was a blanket, along with clean clothes that looked to be roughly the right size to fit me. On top of the pile of folded cloth was a loaf of crusty bread wrapped in thin paper and what looked like a hollow gourd with a cork stopper in the top. There was liquid sloshing inside. I uncorked it and took a sniff. It was odorless, so I stuck my finger inside. Plain water, I was pretty sure.

And that made sense, I supposed. Weren't bread and water supposed to be the standard prisoner rations? I was both hungry and thirsty at this point, too. My last drink had been after the self-defense training with Rans yesterday afternoon, and my last food had been an apple and a banana not much later. I winced at the reminder of the vampire I'd left behind, making an effort to put him out of my mind.

My fingers itched to lift the water to my lips, but memory stopped me. *Doesn't your generation read fairy tales anymore? I mean, is it seriously not common knowledge that you don't eat Fae food or drink Fae wine?*

Albigard had said I was connected to him now because I'd accepted his gift. Suddenly the pile of items looked less like a bounty and more like a trap. I set the water down and stared at it, sitting back on my heels and crossing my arms over my knees.

No one had said anything specifically about accepting Fae clothing or blankets, but I wasn't inclined to take the chance. Nothing I had seen so far indicated that any of them gave a shit about my wellbeing. Why would they do things for my comfort if there wasn't a catch involved somewhere?

I stood up and went to sit against the wall midway between the pile of temptations and the stinking hole. How long would they let me stew in here alone, before they came back and did something worse to me?

I tried to tell myself that being in this cell was a good thing. I tried to tell myself that Albigard was out there somewhere trying to get my dad free right now. Maybe it was like the legal system back home, where you could be held in jail for a long time waiting for a trial. Especially when something as important as an execution was on the line.

That would also be consistent with what Albigard had said about the Court barely being able to come to an agreement on simple issues. It should have been comforting. Instead I felt panic threatening again.

Fucking Christ. What was I doing? What the hell had I *done*? Would I be trapped in here with food I couldn't eat and water I couldn't drink until I died of thirst? If I did give in and eat or drink the Fae gifts, what would happen?

My breathing grew ragged, my heart pounding as a panic attack rose up and took over. I huddled in a ball on the dirt floor at the base of the hollow tree trunk, lightheadedness and nausea fighting for dominance inside me.

Damn it. God*damn* it.

Why couldn't I be strong, like my mother had always been? Strong like Rans? I bet he'd never had a full-on, proper panic attack in his centuries-long life. I tried to breathe through the physical reaction, hearing the raspy gasps echoing louder than they should in the enclosed space. Fuck, I was trapped in here with no doors or windows... fuck fuck *fuck...*

The attack continued for long minutes, measured by the tripping beats of my heart. When it finally subsided, I was trembling, soaked with clammy sweat that beaded chilly and unpleasant on my skin in the cool air of the tree-cell. I covered my face with my hands and shook.

Eventually, I recovered enough to try and think rationally again. The area around me was growing darker and more shadowed as the sun crept across the afternoon sky. I should do a detailed examination of the walls while I could still see my surroundings. Rising on rubbery legs, I placed a hand on the wood next to me and started to feel around, gaining little more than a collection of splinters for my troubles.

Despite the hollowed-out center, the massive tree wasn't rotten. The wood was hard and dense. I picked at a rough area with my thumbnail, and was only able to peel away a tiny sliver before the nail tore. I yelped and sucked on it until the sting subsided.

With the right tools, I could have chipped away at the wall, I was sure... though of course there was no way of knowing whether two inches or two feet of wood lay between me and freedom. And there was also the small matter of my captors not having conveniently left me a hammer and chisel to use—much less a pickaxe.

You should already own these tools, Zorah.

The memory of my father's voice brought an ugly noise to my throat that might have been a bitter laugh, along with a telltale burn at the back of my eyes.

Yeah, thanks Dad. Big help there.

Did I have anything useful with me? Nothing in the pile of supplies was hard or sharp enough to help me with the task. I was wearing jeans, a t-shirt, and sneakers. My belt had a metal buckle on it, but I couldn't think of any way it would be useful.

I caught my breath, my hand flying to my pocket.

I still had my little cell phone. Obviously, relying on cellular service in Dhuinne was a non-starter, but I could at least keep track of the time and have some light once the sun slipped too low in the sky to illuminate my surroundings. I pulled it out and flipped the cover up, powering it on.

Maybe I should have sprung for smartphones when I bought the two burners back in St. Louis, but money had been a real concern at the time. Still, a proper flashlight app would have come in really handy in my current position.

The flip-phone seemed to take longer than it should have to power up. Rather than the usual service provider logo and tinny musical flourish, the screen flickered erratically. Random numbers flashed for a bare instant before the LCD display darkened into blue-black swirls, like someone dropping ink into a glass of water. The screen's illumination flared a final couple of times and died, after which no amount of shaking it or mashing the power button made any difference.

My heart sank, the phone slipping from my numb fingers to drop onto the dirt at my feet. *Fae magic is hard on tech,* Rans had said. Once again, I was reminded of the dashboard clock in Albigard's car, flashing in random, nonsensical segments. It made sense, I supposed—you couldn't get much more exposure to Fae magic than actually being in Dhuinne.

I shivered again, partly because the cool air against my sweaty skin was making me cold, and partly because I would now be stuck in the pitch black if they left me here overnight. The dead phone, my clothing, and the pile of Fae stuff I couldn't use without risking more Bad Things happening constituted the sum total of what I had access to in this place.

I was hungry, thirsty, cold, and I'd barely slept last night. It seemed pretty clear that the most productive thing I could do right now was to try to get some rest in preparation for whatever was going to happen next. I returned to my spot next to the wall, my foot knocking against the abandoned phone in the deepening gloom.

Letting my head tip back, I gazed up at the sky far above me with unfocused eyes. Outside, it was still daylight, though very little of that light now reached the depths of the hollow tree where I was huddled. Even with my arms wrapped around my knees, I was still badly chilled. The woolen blanket tormented me with its presence mere feet away.

How could the Fae possibly know if I was folded up over here, or wrapped around you? it whispered in its stupid imaginary blanket-voice. *Why be cold and miserable if you don't have to be?*

I closed my eyes, cutting off my view of the distant light above. After a few minutes, I scuffled around, pulling my arms inside the armholes of the thin cotton shirt and wrapping them around my middle. It didn't help much.

Rest, I reminded myself. *Try to get some sleep. Maybe something will happen in the morning.*

I kept my eyes stubbornly closed, but rather than shut down, my brain decided that this would be a fantastic time for a rousing game of that old classic, *second-guess every decision you've ever made in your entire life.*

So I did that for a while.

Then I played *what will Rans do when he wakes up to find you gone,* which was no better. Since the two obvious answers were 'shrug and go on like nothing happened,' or 'antagonize every Fae on Earth until he gets himself killed,' it was hard to feel all that great about either possibility.

I'd never been all that good at keeping myself entertained in the absence of any outside help like books, television, or a working phone, so I was definitely struggling under my current circumstances. Chronic anxiety issues tended to do that for you, even when you *weren't* trapped in a living tree-cell with no light and the prospect of execution hanging over your head.

Ha. *'Hanging over your head.'* Decapitation. Sometimes I really slayed myself.

'Slayed.' Right. Double ha.

When I finally gave up and opened my eyes what felt like years later, the sky was dark above me. I quickly closed them again, not liking the fact that I could tell no difference in my surroundings whether my eyelids were open or shut.

It was night. Definitely time to sleep now. *Are you listening, brain?*

More time passed, and I was finally starting to drift when something skittered across the tops of my shoes. I shrieked and scrambled upright in the pitch blackness, leaning a shoulder against the wall to combat my disorientation as I dragged my arms back through my sleeves. Over the sound of my startled breathing, I thought I could hear tiny things rustling in the darkness around me.

But I wasn't going to panic, just because there were mice or… or bugs or something in here with me. I *wasn't*.

Albigard would have mentioned if the Fae executed people by decapitation *or death by hundreds of fucking poisonous nocturnal spiders*. Right? There was food in here with me. Whatever the tiny things were, they probably just wanted the bread.

Something else ran over the toe of my sneaker and I kicked out, unable to stop myself. The unseen activity continued until I was tired of standing, but no way was I going to sit down again while they were in here. I tried to distract myself by figuring out how the things could have gotten in. All I could come up with was the theory that there were tiny tunnels leading from the bottom of the shit-pit, weaving through the tree's roots and leading to the outside world.

That theory made me even less thrilled about the idea of the creepy things touching me than I had been before, which was saying something. The hours crept by, and with unexpected suddenness, the small noises lessened before disappearing completely. When they didn't return after a couple of minutes, I relaxed, and eventually sank back down to sit curled on the floor.

It occurred to me to wonder what had made them decide to leave all at once like that. I had just come to the conclusion that I didn't really care about their motivation as long as they were gone, when the first raindrops splattered down from the opening at the top of the tree.

Oh. Brilliant.

The rain was chilly, and it continued to drip down inside the cell until it had grown into a steady shower. I made my way around the edges of the space—carefully avoiding the shit pit—in hopes of finding a drier area. There was no drier area, however. Rain was falling straight down the hollow trunk and no place was protected. In minutes, I was wet all the way through.

Huddling on the increasingly muddy floor, I shivered my way through the night until the shower eventually stopped. Sometime before morning, exhaustion overcame discomfort and I slid into a sort of fugue state—not quite dozing, but not really awake either.

That lasted until a portal opened without warning in the center of the cell and a glowing ball of light came through it, blinding me. The ball floated up to hover several feet above my head, throwing the damp cell into harsh relief.

When I blinked my eyes back into working order, Caspian was standing over me—staring down at my huddled form with an ugly sneer on his handsome face.

Twelve

Just as Albigard's features had done upon our arrival in Dhuinne, Caspian's features had reverted to their natural elfin appearance. His dark blond brows drew together as he scowled down at me from his towering advantage of height. Their shape might have been different than in his human guise, but the disdain they conveyed was unmistakable.

I scrambled to my feet, my cold, stiff muscles nearly sending me right back to the ground as they cramped. A grimace of pain pulled at my lips as I limped backward, putting as much space as possible between us. It wasn't much.

This is it, I thought as a second Fae stepped out of the portal and closed it behind him. My worst nightmare had come to fruition. I was trapped with my nemesis, completely under his control.

The second Fae looked me over coldly. "It is rather a pitiful creature, is it not?" he asked casually. "I'd honestly expected something a little more impressive."

"Bind it," Caspian ordered, with a dismissive wave in my direction.

"*She,*" I hissed. "Not 'it.' I'm a person, just like the two of you." I let some of my disgust at their nearness creep into my words. "Well… maybe not *just* like you."

The second Fae raised a hand, and an invisible force flung me backward. I hit the damp wood of the wall, my body spread-eagled and the breath knocked out of me.

And I stuck there.

I was pinned to the tree as though someone had coated it with superglue, wheezing as I tried to get my lungs to work. Panic rose, overcoming my bravado in the space of an instant. I couldn't move, I couldn't seem to get a full breath, *and I couldn't get away from them*.

"We will start with a physical examination," Caspian said in a conversational tone, and my mind fled as it had done once before in Albigard's basement.

"Stay away from me," I grated roughly, as power exploded from my center, blasting outward in an invisible wave.

Caspian stumbled back a step, a violent mix of lust and rage sliding across his expression. The wave slid around the second Fae without touching him, though he murmured a startled, *"What in Mab's name*?"

I couldn't pay attention, though—I was instantly locked in a battle of powers with Caspian, who stepped forward like he intended to tear me apart to get at the juicy bits inside. I could feel my succubus nature trying to get its claws into his animus, even though some distant, human part of me was screaming that *no, no*—I didn't *want* that foul and slimy filth inside me.

Before the outcome of the battle could fall in either direction, the other Fae muttered something low and fast, and the same burst of agony I'd felt when Albigard broke my connection with him sliced through me. My muscles jerked against the invisible bonds holding me in place, even as Caspian staggered and caught himself with a hand against the wall next to my head.

He pulled away quickly, as though he'd been burned, and retreated a step. His green eyes flared with outrage. "Ward the creature!" he snarled, turning on his companion. "Why did you not do so immediately?"

"M-my apologies, General," the other Fae stammered. "It appeared harmless—"

My heart was racing at a thousand miles an hour, adrenaline coursing through my system as I struggled fruitlessly against the force holding me to the wall.

"Let me down from here and I'll show you harmless!" I yelled, hating the ugly, hysterical note in my voice.

The second Fae had gone a bit pale, but he murmured again, a glow forming around his right hand. He flicked his fingers at me, the light snaking out and settling around my body in glowing coils before sinking through clothing and skin. My stomach turned over. It felt as though something inside my soul had been cut off… quarantined from the rest of me.

I jerked harder, sore muscles protesting the abuse. "*What did you do?*"

Caspian's hand shot out, backhanding me across the jaw as he'd done in the parking lot in St.

Louis. The sudden pain shocked me into silence. My vision wavered as ringing filled my ears.

"Examine it now," Caspian ordered, his voice coming to me distantly through the haze.

I was only vaguely aware of the other Fae approaching... of his glowing hands splayed as he ran them up and down the length of my body. Not touching, just hovering an inch away. I would've tried to fight against it anyway as the creepy crawly sensation of Fae magic brushed over my skin, but the connection between my mind and body had been temporarily stunned by Caspian's vicious blow. I could taste blood on my tongue.

"Well?" Caspian asked impatiently, after his companion had run his hands over every part of me.

"It appears to be a normal human, General," he said, his voice filled with deference, as though he knew that wasn't the answer Caspian wanted.

"'*She*,'" I insisted in a hoarse croak, only to be completely ignored.

"A *normal human*?" The words dripped with disdain. "And that disgusting display a few minutes ago was something one would find in a *normal human*, was it?"

The underling cleared his throat. "Clearly not, General. As you said earlier, that is a demonic attribute, but I am certain the creature is not a true cambion. I have no explanation."

The ringing in my skull was subsiding, dizziness giving way to a throbbing ache in my jaw that pulsed in time with my heartbeat. I wanted to shake my head in an attempt to clear it further, but

I couldn't even move that much, bound to the wall as I was.

"Then *find* an explanation!" Caspian demanded. "Why do you think I brought you here in the first place? Somehow, the demons have discovered a way to seed their filth through more than a single generation. I must know what it is."

His companion hesitated. "The only approach I can think of which might be effective would be delving directly into the core of its magical nature. It would take extensive time and energy, and I can't guarantee that the creature would not be permanently damaged, depending on the depth at which its magic lies and the amount of protection around it."

Caspian sneered. "Do it."

And with that careless command began the worst experience of my twenty-six years of life. Worse than my father's cold dismissal. Worse than knowing I'd betrayed Rans' trust in order to protect him. Worse than the feeling as I stepped through the gate between Earth and Dhuinne with the sure knowledge that I would never see home again.

Worse than seeing my mother killed.

A week ago, I had no idea that magic existed inside me at all. I thought I was normal, at least for a given definition of normal—a sickly, slightly messed up woman with a tragic past, who never really fit in anywhere. Now, I was about to learn the lengths my body would go to in an attempt to protect the magic inside me from attack by an outsider.

I had no frame of reference for what Caspian's spell-wielding underling was doing, beyond the few instances I'd seen of Fae magic being performed to make portals, change a person's appearance, or restrain someone. At first, he retreated to the far side of the cramped cell and turned away. His head was bowed, and I could hear him muttering more mysterious words. A faint glow began to emanate from his entire body.

My attention was caught between whatever he was doing, and my instinctive feeling of repulsion as Caspian stared at me like he could peel back the layers of my clothing and skin with his eyes. When Fae Two turned to face me again and came closer, he was still surrounded by that pale halo of light.

I braced myself, not knowing what I was bracing against. The light gathered into a bright point in the center of the Fae's forehead—the place one of my yoga instructors called the third eye. I tried to flinch back as the glow began to pour out of him and toward me, but there was no place for me to go.

At first, I felt nothing when it touched me in the same place on my forehead and sank into my skin. Then, I felt warmth. Then, tingling. The tingling became burning, and the burning became a metal spike driving through my skull.

"Stop resisting, demonkin," my Fae tormenter said through gritted teeth. "You will only damage yourself."

It was the first time he'd addressed me directly, but somehow I couldn't get too excited about it with his creepy magic drilling a hole through my head.

"I'm not doing a damn thing, you fucker," I snarled. "Stop hurting me!"

He didn't stop.

All sense of time disappeared as the magical probing continued. It grew more insistent as the Fae evidently failed to get whatever the hell he was after. I could track his growing frustration by the amount of pain I was in, and I had a horrible suspicion that what felt like hours of agony had in reality been only moments.

When my head didn't yield whatever information he was after, the attack moved to a spot at the base of my neck. I was already desperately thirsty, my throat dry and aching. Now, it was on fire. I choked, trying to force air past the furnace blocking my trachea as I squirmed and writhed in a useless panic.

"The bloodsucker has fed from her neck recently," came the Fae's distant voice. "More than once, I think."

"What do I care about that?" Caspian snapped from someplace to my right. "It has no bearing on how she originally came to exist. Keep going!"

For some reason, it enraged me that Fae Two could know something like that about me without me telling him. The anger tangled with my panic at not being able to breathe properly. I tried to snarl, to yell and curse at them both, but the attempt only set me to choking harder. My lungs burned and seized until I was sure I would pass out, but before that happened, the magical attack moved lower.

Now, the Fae's magic focused on the center of my breastbone, sinking through skin and bone to wrap around my heart. I tried to drag air past the sandpaper ruin of my throat, while my pulse skipped and thudded like a heart attack victim's. My tormenter might as well be driving a blade into the beating flesh… or wrapping it in barbed wire that ripped into the muscle with every throb.

I still didn't have enough air to yell, but a terrible groan wrenched free from my throat. The torture continued until I was sure my heart must be a burned and bleeding mass of gristle inside my chest, managing only one beat out of every two or three I should have felt. I hung from the wall, more pathetic noises choking free from my lips, wishing desperately that I were a vampire so I wouldn't have to feel my tortured heart fighting to pump blood and life through my body.

The flow of magic moved yet again, settling into position over my navel and flowing inside to twist my guts into knots. I retched, bile clawing its way up my abused throat, though there was almost nothing in my stomach after well over a day without food or water. The agony in my intestines made me lightheaded, but through the vertigo and disorientation, something clicked into place as I remembered thinking about my yoga instructor earlier. The Fae was attacking my chakra points, from top to bottom. Which meant that next—

The burning magic moved lower, wrapping around the place deep inside me that throbbed and pulled at Rans' animus when we were together. The place that sucked at other people's energy and dragged it into me to sustain me. The Fae probed and squeezed, trying to draw out the secrets buried there.

All of my muscles started jerking like a palsy victim's, and a horrible, high-pitched noise slipped free of my lips.

"It is still resisting, General." I was barely aware of the strain coloring the Fae's voice as my body fought against the intrusion.

"Push harder!" Caspian's words sounded blurred around the edges as my hearing faded in and out.

The sensation intensified, and I screamed, forcing the sound past my ruined throat, heedless of the additional agony it caused. I screamed and screamed, and kept screaming until darkness closed around the edges of my vision and my hearing faded away to nothing.

I was barely aware of the magical bindings holding me to the wall disappearing some unknown amount of time later. Then I was falling, and the final sparks of consciousness deserted me before the impact of my body hitting the packed dirt floor registered.

Thirteen

Thirst. That was the first thing that registered when I next regained awareness of my surroundings. I thought I'd known what it felt like to be thirsty after spending hot and humid St. Louis afternoons outside in the baking sun. I thought I'd known what it felt like to be hungry after sometimes skipping breakfast and lunch because I was running late and had work to catch up at MMHA.

I'd been a fool.

My body was howling at me… wailing in the same way my voice had been wailing as Caspian's underling pulled and hacked at my succubus powers with his magic. This was the kind of thirst that killed. The kind of hunger that made humans into ravenous animals. I imagined that plane crash victims who turned to cannibalism to survive felt hunger like this as they looked at their victims' bodies.

At first, I thought it was the ache of thirst that roused me from unconsciousness. But that wasn't it. Cold rain was falling into the tree-trunk cell again, as though to taunt me. With a hoarse groan, I managed to flop onto my back. I stretched my mouth open as wide as I could, the occasional cool splatter falling against my tongue.

My shoulder had bumped against something when I rolled over. Lightning flashed, briefly illuminating my darkened surroundings, and I saw the water-gourd along with a freshly wrapped parcel that must be more bread lying next to me. My stomach cramped with need.

Could drinking and eating the Fae gifts possibly make things worse than they were already? What could happen to me that would be worse than what had already happened? Worse than the terrible, tender pain inside me where my tormenter had tried to tear part of me out by the roots? I would die if I didn't get more water than the steady drizzle could provide.

Tears tried to spring to my eyes and I blinked them back ruthlessly, unwilling to waste whatever small reserves of moisture remained in my body. I pictured Caspian leering down at me, waiting with glee for my resolve to break. Anger flared like a raging fire, and I struck out with my arm. The impact knocked the gourd across the cell. I heard water glugging—either the container had cracked or the cork had come out, and now the water was seeping away to join the raindrops in the dirt below me.

Temptation removed.

I knocked the bread away next, though it didn't roll very far. It didn't matter. Even if the drizzle had dampened it through its paper wrapper, I was pretty sure I couldn't swallow it successfully without some liquid to moisten my mouth and throat first.

My body shuddered from a combination of cold and exhaustion. The mud I was lying on leached the heat from my muscles, and I felt like I'd been awake for days despite the long hours I'd apparently spent unconscious. My chattering teeth aggravated the pounding headache throbbing behind my temples. I opened my mouth again to the rain to stop my teeth repeatedly crashing against each other.

I tried to take stock. It was difficult for me to feel much about my succubus nature when I wasn't actively drawing animus from someone. For an instant, my mind flashed back to Rans, his eyes closed in ecstasy as he came inside me; the feeling of complete safety and satisfaction I'd felt in his arms on the handful of occasions after we'd pleasured each other. Again, tears pricked behind my eyes, stinging like acid.

Had Caspian and his lackey succeeded at whatever they'd been trying to do to me? I didn't think so. If they'd really ripped out my magic somehow, that part of me wouldn't feel so tender and abused. At least, that's what I was going to continue telling myself.

I kept my mouth wide open to the rain as I pondered, hoping that only water would fall into it and not, y'know, bird poop or something. But now the shower was easing off, and the steady *drip-drip-drip* had barely been enough to wet my mouth, much less for me to swallow any appreciable amount of it.

Out of sheer desperation, I marshaled what strength I could and scooted around until my face was pressed against the wall. It was damp from the rivulets of rain dripping down, so I started licking. Not even the threat of splinters in my tongue was enough to discourage me from lapping up every resin-flavored drop of moisture I could reach.

A brief flash of worry that Fae rain might still count as a gift flickered across my thoughts, but it was clear the rain had been meant as another torment rather than a blessing. Besides, it was too late. Once the first drop slid across my tongue, it was done, one way or another.

Too late, it occurred to me that the cessation of the rain might herald something else. By necessity, I'd let my body fall back to the ground once I'd licked up all the moisture I could reach from the wall. My shivering was bad enough that I didn't notice the return of my invisible, scurrying companions from the previous night until one skittered across the bare skin of my hand.

I would've shrieked, but all that emerged from my dry throat was a choked wheeze. Suddenly, they were all over me, and I was too weak to lunge to my feet and shake them off—whatever they were. I tried to flail, but just ended up flopping around a bit like a broken marionette. Panic clawed at me, the instinctive human fear of small things with scurrying legs.

The bread, I remembered. *They were probably after the bread, not me.*

Focusing what little strength I had, I shuffled toward where I thought the bread had ended up and felt around until my forearm brushed it, trying to ignore the scuttling around me. I grabbed the loaf, gritting my teeth when several *somethings* wriggled out from beneath my grip. I'd been right—the paper wrapping was gone and I could feel holes eaten through the crust.

I threw it across the cell, hearing a soft *thump-plop* noise. Though I hadn't been trying to, I must've slam-dunked it right into the shit-pit. The idea was a bit stomach-turning, but I stopped caring about that when—a few moments later—all of the sounds of rustling headed for that side of the hollow tree and stayed there.

Whatever the things were, I hoped they all came down with horrible *E. coli* infections and died before morning.

With the excitement evidently over, I lay trembling on the ground in a fetal position, wishing desperately that I could fall asleep and knowing it was completely hopeless. As I had the previous night, I drifted in and out of a semi-aware state, dreading what the morning might bring.

Unsurprisingly, the morning brought Caspian's return. A portal sizzled into existence, dragging my fractured awareness back to the here-and-now. The floating ball of light whizzed through, dazzling my exhausted eyes, and Caspian followed.

He did not make the gesture I'd noticed other Fae use to close the portal, but it snapped shut behind him nonetheless. I forced my sluggish mind to think back over my unpleasant association with the man in front of me, connections slipping into place.

I ran my tongue over the roof of my mouth, testing whether I had enough saliva to speak. "Where's your torture expert this morning, Golden Boy?" I rasped.

Caspian's eyes took in the cracked water gourd lying at the base of the wall before returning to me with a look of utter contempt. I could imagine what he was seeing—muddy clothing, bruised jaw, red eyes, cracked lips.

"He'll be along in a few minutes to pick up where we left off yesterday," the Fae said. His lips twisted as though addressing me directly left a bad taste in his mouth. "I came ahead to explain what awaits you if you continue to resist Reefe's attempts to scrive your magical core."

I stared at him, willing myself not to break eye contact. "You can't do magic, can you?" I asked in a hoarse voice. "Not the shiny, exciting kind, anyway. That wasn't even your portal just now, was it?"

If not for the faint tightening at the edge of his jaw, I'd have thought he was ignoring my words completely.

"Today," he continued, "we will not waste more time beating around the bush. The source of your foul energy is clear enough. I will find out what lies beneath the demon taint, if I have to tear pieces of you out by the roots one-by-one to do so."

"But it won't be you doing the tearing, now will it?" I shot back. "You have to bring in someone else to help with that part. What's the deal? Did you spend too much time playing human on Earth, or something? Though that didn't seem to stop Albigard from being a magical badass—"

Caspian stepped forward until he was looming over me. Idly, I wished for enough strength to swing a foot up and kick him in the nuts. Did Fae have testicles? I hoped I'd have a chance to find out before I died.

"Once your broken body has given up the last of its secrets, you will be taken away and euthanized like the misbegotten beast you are. I shall take great satisfaction in watching the surprise on your face as your decapitated head hits the ground and rolls away."

I peered up at him, my weakness making me strangely numb to fear. "What did I ever do to piss on your cornflakes, Caspian? I mean... *seriously*."

Caspian drew breath—to answer, or maybe to spit on me. I wasn't sure. Before he could do either, though, the portal opened again and Fae Two stepped through, closing it behind him with a wave. I took some slight satisfaction in the fact that he looked like shit, at least for a Fae—way less unruffled and iridescent than his boss, for instance. Instead, he looked flustered and like he was in need of a good night's sleep.

Caspian subsided, stepping away to address his underling instead. "Don't bother binding it to the wall today," he said. "I think the filth on the floor will do just fine for such a creature."

Did the second Fae look a bit troubled at that, or was I just imagining things? It didn't matter. A moment later, a wave of magic hit me, gluing me to the damp, chilly mud as effectively as I'd been pinned to the wall yesterday.

"I really, really hate this, you know," I told the floating ball of light hovering above the ugly tableau the three of us made.

Next came the warding coils, and then, the pain. Caspian hadn't been lying—Fae Two—or Reefe, or whatever he was called—went straight for the place in my pelvis that still ached from the previous day's torture. The feeling yanked fresh screams from my throat, just as it had before. But even after the pitiful amount of rainwater I'd managed to lick up, I was still most of a day further along in the process of dying of thirst.

And I have to say, trying to scream while being physically unable to do more than wheeze and choke might just be the most horrible feeling a human being is capable of experiencing. Because while Caspian and his cronies considered me nothing more than a monstrous mistake, in my head, I was still just a human girl who'd been dragged headfirst into something far, far beyond her depth.

"We can keep this up all day if necessary, demonkin," Caspian growled.

Fuck you, I mouthed silently… right before I passed out again.

I awoke alone. The sky above me was light rather than dark this time, though I couldn't have said whether it was later on the same day or the following day. My vision was blurry, and trying to clear it somehow seemed like far too much work to be worthwhile.

For several minutes, I thought they must have left me magically bound to the floor, because my arms and legs didn't respond when I thought about moving them. Then, I realized I really was just *that* battered and weak. With a concentrated effort, I lifted my head to look around the cell.

Empty. They hadn't even left me bread and water this time.

Yeah, Zorah... wow. Way to go. You really showed them, didn't you?

The snide inner voice was irrelevant, though. I couldn't have moved from my position and sat up to eat or drink it anyway. The deeply buried human instinct that tells you when you're about to die was chiming *too late, too late, too late* in a repetitive internal refrain.

I was done. I couldn't fight anymore—not that fighting had gained me anything useful to this point. Idly, I wondered if Reefe had managed to succeed this time at whatever he was trying to do to me.

Then a portal opened, and a raspy groan emerged from my lips, unbidden.

No. I didn't want to do this anymore.

Please, no more.

Fourteen

I flinched backward when a figure stepped out of the portal. When I blinked against the awful sandpapery feel of my eyelids, my vision eventually cleared enough to see that it wasn't Caspian or his underling, and I relaxed marginally. I was still sprawled on the floor next to the rough wood of the wall, and I looked up from beneath the messy tangle of my hair with wary eyes. A second Fae joined the first—guards, I thought, although I didn't recognize either of their faces.

"Get the thing on its feet and clean the filth off its clothes," the first one muttered. "*Mab's garden*, the stench it gives off is foul. Did we piss someone off to get these orders, or what?"

If I thought I'd have been able to manage more than a croak, I might've made some quip like, *'Stench? Yeah, that tends to happen when you lock someone up inside a tree and torment them for days.'*

"*Her,*" I rasped instead. "Not *'it.'*"

Fuck, why was I even bothering? What possible benefit did I expect to gain from the effort?

Indeed, the guards eyeballed me like I was stinking vermin that had just stood up and demanded voting rights. Neither of them responded, merely dragging me upright by the biceps.

It hurt every bit as much as I'd expected it to. How could muscles and joints throb with so much agony without tearing and shattering to pieces? I moaned, choking on the noise. Then the choking tore at my roiling stomach, making me retch. There wasn't even enough moisture left inside me for bile to come up at this point.

"Try giving it the water," said the second one. "See if that shuts it up."

The other one removed one of the weird water-gourd things from a strap over his shoulder and uncorked it, thrusting the opening toward my mouth. I groaned again and clenched my eyes shut. *Jesus.* At what point had I gotten so thirsty that I could actually *smell water* when it was nearby?

I bit the inside of my cheek hard. There was some reason I shouldn't drink this. It was important. Important enough that I'd dumped the last water they'd sent me onto the dirt floor. What was it? Why the hell had I done that instead of slaking my thirst?

Oh. Right.

Faerie food and faerie drink. Faerie gifts… accept them and you gave the faeries a way to control you… or something. I'd drunk Albigard's mead, and now he could find me anywhere.

But did it really matter anymore? The Fae already controlled me. They already had me, and soon they would kill me—if I didn't die of thirst before then. I could feel my mouth trying and failing to salivate at the prospect of drinking something. Eating something. The thought of that cool liquid sliding across my tongue and down my throat was like a siren song.

Only one thing held me back. What if Caspian had sent it? What if it was *his* gift? I swiped out weakly, fresh pain exploding through my body as I knocked the gourd out of the guard's surprised grip. It hit the ground and splashed across our feet and lower legs.

"Animal!" he growled, and hit me across the face.

My head jerked sideways and the room swayed, but beyond that the impact barely registered amongst my body's clamoring distress. Maybe I could absorb some of the water soaking my filthy jeans via osmosis. Or would that still count as consuming Fae drink?

"Enough," said the other guard. "Let's just deliver it before the Court like we're supposed to. I can't get away from it fast enough, honestly."

Feeling's mutual, asshole.

The guard holding me grunted. "Yeah. Filthy creature. Can you even imagine letting a demon fuck you? Much less carrying demon-spawn around for months and actually *birthing it*. Humans are so disgusting."

God, I wanted to spit at them. I wanted to lift my chin and deliver a cutting verbal smackdown that would leave them smarting for days. I wanted to be a badass faerie-killing assassin and overpower them… take their weapons… leap through the open portal and fuck up every Fae standing between me and wherever they were keeping my father now.

Instead, I stood on shaky legs, my body trembling so hard it threatened to send me straight back down to the ground, feeling the burn behind my eyeballs that meant I'd be crying like a little bitch if I wasn't too dehydrated to make tears.

"Go to hell," I managed, more the shape of the words than an actual sound.

The second guard only made a sound of disgust. One of them muttered a new spell, and my damp, muddy clothing instantly dried, the dirt flaking away. Between them, the pair hauled me through the portal to whatever lay on the other side. And what lay on the other side was one of those big, official-looking buildings with plants and flowers choking the interior, like the place we'd met with the Recorder. It might've been the same building or a different one. With all the vines and leaves everywhere, it was impossible to tell.

I was dragged inside. A pair of double doors loomed in front of us, flanked by more stony faced guards. Their eyes flicked over me and the one on the right said, "You're expected. Take the thing inside. They're ready to begin."

What few functioning brain cells I possessed were starting to fire intermittently. Maybe this was it. This looked like the kind of building in which you might sentence someone to be executed. Maybe I'd be out of Caspian's reach soon.

Sudden worry pricked at me. I still didn't know what had become of my father. He needed care. Medical care, psychological care. He needed to be on Earth, not this terrible and astonishing place inhabited by beautiful monsters. I had to pull myself together enough that I could at least speak. I needed to be able to ask what had happened to him… to beg for his freedom in exchange for my life, if the chance arose.

The doors swung open, but I still couldn't do more than croak. My throat was as dry as the Sahara no matter how many times I tried to swallow.

The chamber beyond made me certain that I was right about where we were. Like so many things on Dhuinne, it was different in subtle ways from anything I was familiar with on Earth, while still clearly announcing its purpose. This was a courtroom. Or perhaps more accurately, a Courtroom. If I was right, I had finally come face to face with the Fae Court.

The place was spectacular. As with so much of Dhuinne, it, too, was choked with living things, the invading plants almost appearing to move as they battled and strained to grow longer, lusher, more colorful than their neighbors. The room was delineated clearly into three zones. The far end was raised on a platform a couple of feet above the area inside the double doors. But the raised area was also divided down the middle, separating the left and right sides of the dais. Each side held a long wooden seating area like a judge's bench.

An open area lay in front of the split dais. The guards hauled me toward it, passing pew-like seats on either side of the aisle we were traversing. The seats were mostly full from what I could see through all the leaves. The pews held a mix of people, while the raised sections at the front appeared segregated by sex—females on the right and males on the left.

My shoes fell soundlessly on more of the weird Fae moss—the blue-green of the natural carpet broken here and there by tiny white flowers poking through. I'd heard the low murmur of people talking amongst themselves when the doors first opened to admit my guards, but the chamber became very quiet the moment the Fae inside noticed my arrival.

The guards dumped me in the empty area at the base of the platform, and without their support, my knees crumpled immediately. At least the moss made for a soft landing, though I felt strangely bad about having crushed some of the little white flowers.

"The prisoner, as requested, Honored Ones," said the guard on my left, as both bowed low.

One of the male Fae on the raised platform stood, looking down his nose at me. My heart stuttered and sped up as I recognized Caspian, dressed now in fine robes rather than the utilitarian clothing I'd grown used to seeing over the past couple of days.

"Why is the creature not restrained?" he demanded, contempt dripping from his words.

The female Fae in the centermost seat on that side of the dais spoke in a dry voice. "Perhaps because she is clearly too weakened to do anything, including stand up."

I wasn't sure if the undercurrent of amusement beneath the words irritated me or relieved me, but at least she hadn't referred to me as an 'it.' I focused on her as best I could, hoping that the distraction would stop me from panicking over Caspian's presence. She was as beautiful as Albigard and Caspian were handsome, with pale skin and threads of golden chain shaping her fiery red hair into an artful tumble of curls.

My nerves were just about at their breaking point after the last couple of days, but oddly, I didn't seem to have the same instinctive aversion to the female Fae gathered on the right side of the platform as I did to the males I'd met.

A distant buzzing noise was overtaking my hearing again as my brief burst of adrenaline faded, rendering the conversation between Caspian and the woman a meaningless jumble of sounds. I craned around, trying to get a better read on the people seated in the lower part of the room.

The audience, I thought bitterly, picturing a bunch of seventeenth century peasants gathering to watch the casual entertainment of a witch trial. They weren't all peasants, though—my eyes fell on Albigard sitting on one of the benches in the front row. His gaze flicked over me as though I was only of the barest interest to him.

I was way too far gone to try and figure out if there was any danger in letting the people here see us interacting, or if he just didn't give a shit now that he'd delivered me into the Court's hands. I stared at him fixedly for the space of several heartbeats, but his face was a smooth mask, mirror-like in its cool perfection.

I looked away when movement from the front pew on the other side of the aisle caught in my peripheral vision—a small, dark form. Distant surprise prickled at me as I recognized—of all things—the cat from the cottage where Dad was being kept. Or, at the very least, a nearly identical cat—black with a diamond-shaped patch of white on its chest, and slanted green eyes.

Of course, the presence of a cat in a courtroom might just be proof that I was finally losing it. Not really a stretch at this point, I supposed. *Christ.* Could this just be over soon, please?

Light flared behind me. I turned to face the dais again with a choked gasp of fear, as the glow of magic lit one of the red-haired woman's hands. She flicked it toward me carelessly, but I was too weak to even attempt to scuttle out of its way like some pathetic insect.

The ball of light sank into my chest before I could do more than draw breath. The familiar itchiness crawled across me, but no pain followed. Instead, energy suffused my limbs. I swallowed, finally able to work up a bit of saliva—my throat clicking audibly as the buzzing, ringing noise in my ears subsided.

"—that better, demonkin?" the woman asked, raising a swept eyebrow at me.

"W-what did you do?" I rasped, climbing unsteadily to my feet.

The magic conveyed the same sense of artificial wellbeing that you sometimes got from heavy-duty painkillers—not the cheap over-the-counter stuff. The sense of your body being on borrowed time, feeling all right but not really *all right.*

"Nothing of import," said the woman. "This would be a sad excuse for a Court if the subject were unable to speak and answer questions."

"Thank you," I said cautiously. "I think."

Caspian narrowed his eyes. "I protest this waste of resources on a creature that should not exist in the first place."

"Yes," the woman replied. "You've made that quite clear, Caspian. However, while the Unseelie may run the overkeeps on Earth, the Seelie still have the final say on Dhuinne."

Oh, good, I thought. *Politics. Exactly what I needed today.*

"So, is this like a trial, then?" I asked, trying to draw the woman out since it seemed like she was way less of a bigot than most of the other Fae I'd dealt with so far.

"No, demonkin," she said. "What reason would we have to place you on trial? This is the meeting to determine our response to the treaty violation perpetrated by our enemies."

"And what about me?" I tried. "I'm just as much a victim of this treaty violation as anyone else. More so, even."

At least that got a reaction, muttering erupting around the chamber. Caspian made a derisive noise.

"You are a mistake," he said. "One which we will take pleasure in erasing."

Aaand, there it was. Not that I had truly held out hope of anything different.

I kept my eyes on the woman. "You're going to kill me in cold blood, even though I've never done a damned thing to any of you."

She did not break my gaze, and I imagined I caught the faintest whiff of regret in her reply. "Your life poses an existential threat to our people. The demons cannot be allowed to use humans as breeding stock, to swell their ranks and tip the balance of power."

"Must we waste time cosseting this abomination, Magistrate?" grumbled another of the male Fae seated above me. "The question is not about the demonkin's fate. It is about the sanctions we can apply toward those who spawned it."

"Wait!" I said, sensing I was losing my brief connection with the red-haired Fae. "If you're going to kill me, I have a request first! My father—"

She cut me off. "The Court will discuss the disposition of your sire in due course, child. That matter is under review, since no sign of demon taint could be found in him."

"Beyond the taint of letting a cambion touch him!" someone jeered from the crowd behind me.

Rage and despair swirled inside me, forming a bitter slurry.

"Silence," the Magistrate said evenly, and the undercurrent of muttering died down.

I ignored the order, since I figured they could only chop my head off once. "If my father is free of... *taint*—" I spit the word out as if it tasted bad. "—then let him go back to Earth! Something's wrong with him! He needs help, the kind he can only get from other humans—"

"Must we listen to more of this bleating, Magistrate?" Caspian asked, his mouth twisting as though he'd tasted something sour. "The Court has seen for itself the truth of the creature's nature. If you will not allow me more time to study it, then take it away to be dealt with. Letting it linger like this is cruel, would you not agree?"

He sneered, the corners of his eyes crinkling at me.

"*Bastard,*" I whispered, and those eyes turned hard and flat.

The Magistrate sighed. "I suppose you're right, General. Guardsmen, take the demonkin to the execution block and ensure that she is dispatched cleanly. Have the remains taken to the healers for further study."

Gooseflesh chased itself across my skin, and a wave of dizziness washed over me. The guards stepped forward from their positions at the corners of the room. A crazy impulse told me to run, or maybe to lunge for Caspian and try to claw his bastard eyes out with my fingernails while I still had the chance.

Before I could do more than draw in a breath—to rage, to scream, to curse every Fae in this room—the double doors at the back of the chamber slammed inward. I whirled, nearly tripping over my own feet as I fought weakness and vertigo.

Blinking rapidly, I stared open-mouthed at the dark figure striding into the court, blue eyes blazing and leather coat billowing behind him. Moss blackened and curled beneath his boots as he passed, the vines and flowers around him withering in his wake. Cries of alarm erupted around the room as several of the Fae on the dais surged to their feet.

"Actually, guardsmen," Rans said, "I would strongly advise against that course of action."

Fifteen

Either the impossible had just happened, or my mind had just snapped. The latter option seemed a lot more likely, somehow. I continued to stare in bewilderment, my mouth gaping like I was a particularly dull-witted fish. And okay, maybe I hadn't lost my mind, because the guards that had been heading for me stopped in their tracks with similarly shocked expressions on their faces.

Rans didn't slow down until he reached me, his eyes glowing and his fangs bared. Without a word, he grabbed my hand and raised my wrist to his lips.

"What is the meaning of this?" the Magistrate demanded with what I had to admit was admirable steadiness.

I was still mired in shock, wondering if Rans was about to kiss the delicate skin on my inner wrist—right up until his fangs tore into my flesh. I cried out... a stupid, pathetic squeak. What the hell? Was I hallucinating after all?

His throat worked as he swallowed, and then he was reaching into his pocket with his free hand, pulling out something small and sharp edged, like a piece of milky quartz. He slapped my still-bleeding wrist against it.

"What is that crystal?" Caspian demanded. "Guards, stop him!"

"Rans, what the hell?" I tried.

But Rans had already dropped my arm. His fangs tore into the flesh at the base of his thumb, a gout of red erupting in front of my wavering vision. He placed the bloody wound over my mouth, and I made a shocked noise as coppery liquid seeped between my open lips.

"If you want to get out of here alive, swallow," he said in a voice too low to be heard by anyone else.

I'm sure my eyes were bugging out of my head as salty blood coated my tongue. My empty stomach tried to flip over as repulsion at the idea of someone else's blood in my mouth warred with my body's survival instincts... and lost. This was liquid, and I had nearly died of thirst. Suddenly, I could sympathize with desperate shipwreck victims who succumbed to the deadly lure of drinking seawater.

I swallowed.

"No!" Caspian roared, and vaulted over the long wooden desk he'd been seated behind, sending piles of papers flying in his wake.

The guards were still hesitating a few steps away. Rans smeared his blood over the mysterious crystal, mixing it with mine. The crystal glowed, turning ruby red. I watched, dumbfounded, as he tossed the thing onto the moss-covered floor and crushed it with a boot heel. The ruby-colored light exploded outward as the crystal shattered. I felt it pass through me like a power surge.

Caspian slid to a halt at the edge of the dais. Everyone in the chamber seemed to have gone very still all of the sudden. I was still gaping, queasily aware of Rans' blood smeared across my lips.

He straightened, addressing his next words to the Magistrate. The female Fae had risen in alarm with the others, but unlike Caspian she'd made no move to approach us.

"I declare that this woman shares my life-bond," Rans said, his voice carrying to every corner of the chamber. "Her soul is now tied to mine. Killing her kills me as well." He lifted his hands as though baring himself to attack. "There you are, then, mates. I've made it easy for you. Two for one. Anyone want to have a go?"

I stared at him. What the… *what*?

Nobody moved.

Eventually, the Magistrate sat down again in slow motion, her green eyes raking over the rest of the Court. The others followed suit, returning to their chairs—all except for Caspian, who still stood poised on the edge of the dais, his chest rising and falling fast.

His eyes glared daggers at us.

I swallowed hard, scrubbing at my face and mouth with the back of my hand. Unfortunately, my hand was bloody, too, and all of it was starting to dry on my skin. At least that meant the wounds from Rans' fangs were already closed over, I supposed. Beneath our feet, the circle of blackened, dying moss and flowers continued to spread slowly outward.

"No one?" Rans taunted. "Really? Last surviving member of your sworn enemies, barging right into the seat of power on Dhuinne, and none of you want a go at me?"

A tendon jerked in Caspian's jaw.

"If anyone feels like explaining what the hell is going on, that would be freakin' awesome as far as I'm concerned," I said.

The Magistrate didn't even look at me. Her eyes narrowed, her attention staying firmly on Rans.

"Your continued survival is mandated within a clause of the peace treaty, vampire," she said slowly.

"Yeah, see, I thought it must be something like that," Rans muttered.

"The demons have already broken the treaty!" Caspian snarled, gesturing at me. "The proof stands right in front of us!"

Rans narrowed his eyes. "Oh? Well, it sounds like the peace is over, then. What a terrible pity. I suppose you'd better come down here and stake me through the heart. Just think, Golden Boy—all of your problems solved with a single blow."

Somehow, I couldn't believe that antagonizing the powerful guy who seemed to hate both our guts was that great of a plan—but then again, I was the girl who'd walked into Dhuinne with every expectation that I'd be beheaded for my troubles. So maybe I didn't have much room to talk.

"That can be arranged, parasite," Caspian said.

I tensed as Rans drew himself up straight and pushed me behind him, but the Magistrate's voice rang out before Caspian could jump down from the platform.

"Hold!"

Caspian stood poised, his fists clenching and unclenching in poorly suppressed rage.

"Sit *down*, General," the Magistrate continued. "This body will not respond to a single criminal act from half a century ago by committing an officially sanctioned treaty violation in open Court."

I held my breath, trying rather desperately to drag my wits together and catch up with whatever the fuck was happening around me. I still felt like a wreck, though perhaps not as much of a wreck as I should have been. I had no idea what the Magistrate had done to me with her glowy magic hands, or how long it would last. But—disgusting though it might be—it made a sort of twisted sense that if vampire blood healed human wounds, swallowing it would give your health an even bigger boost than applying it topically.

Meanwhile, Rans still seemed intent on heckling Caspian into trying to kill both of us.

"Well, Golden Boy? You heard the lady. What's it going to be?" he pressed.

Maybe possessing two X-chromosomes trumped species differences, because the Magistrate sounded like she was even closer to the end of her tether than I was—and at this point, that was saying something.

"You presume much, vampire," she said. "Perhaps you would do better to enjoy your strategic victory without attempting to goad members of this Court into violence. You have what you apparently wanted—though I don't claim to understand your motives. We cannot execute the part-breed now that her life is tied to yours."

Caspian was still hanging onto his self-control by a thread, it seemed. A slow smile stretched his features… a smile I really didn't like.

"Perhaps not," he said. "But nothing prevents us from imprisoning the creature here for further study, Magistrate. As long as it doesn't die, no harm comes to the bloodsucker, and by extension, the treaty."

An icy wave of cold shuddered through my body, and I had to stop myself from cringing at the words. Rans' hand shot out to hold me in place.

"By all means, try to take her away from me," he said, biting off the words. "See if you can do it without killing me during the attempt."

"Enough!" the Magistrate snapped. "All of this is uncalled for. You may leave here with the part-breed, as long as you do so peacefully… and *promptly*."

Several of the Unseelie shifted in their seats, exchanging unhappy murmurs.

"I'd love to, thanks," Rans said. "Now, give the two of us an escort back to the gate to Earth, so none of the guards between here and there get any ideas above their station. Then we'll be on our way."

After the events of the past several minutes, I'd almost forgotten about Albigard's presence here, but at those words he rose from his seat and made to step toward us. Rans turned at the movement, his body freezing into dangerous stillness.

"No," he growled, his eyes flashing murder. "Not you."

Albigard paused, green gaze locking with blue for a long moment before he consciously relaxed his spine and shrugged, as though it was nothing to him either way. After a tense few beats while the other Fae in the room looked nervously at each other, wondering if anyone else would step up, the large black cat hopped down from its perch and trotted past us toward the double doors, its tail held high.

I was already pretty much maxed out when it came to weird, but Rans just muttered, "That works, I suppose," and headed after the animal, my bloody hand clasped in his.

I tagged along behind him, trying to decide if this was really happening or not. Was I about to surface from unconsciousness, only to find myself still lying on the hard-packed dirt floor inside the tree-cell? Or had the whole thing been a dream from the start, and I would wake up to find that I'd drifted off in Tom and Glynda's bedroom in Chicago?

I shuddered at the idea that I might still have to face sneaking out of the house, calling Albigard and talking him into helping me after this nightmare. But… that would mean seeing my dad had been a dream, too. It would mean he wasn't actually damaged. It would mean he hadn't really talked to me like I was something to be tossed aside and forgotten.

Shit.

Shit, shit, shit.

I was losing it, my feet stumbling over nothing as my mind whirled in tighter and tighter circles. Rans pulled me closer to him, tucking me against his body and wrapping an arm around my shoulders.

The double doors were still open after his dramatic entrance earlier. The cat padded past the dumbfounded guards, and we followed right behind. Indeed, the whole place seemed to have come to a crashing halt after the unexpected spectacle in the courtroom, with Fae staring at us like they were afraid Rans might draw a hidden weapon and start randomly hacking away at them.

Was it an irrational fear? I had absolutely no fucking clue.

"Portal," Rans said, once the three of us had exited the building. "She's too weak to walk back."

My fractured attention had been caught by the trail of dead and decomposing vines in our wake, Dhuinne's magical plant life succumbing to Rans' undead aura. Or something. Maybe that was why it took me longer than it should have to realize he was talking to the animal, not me.

"But... it's just a cat..." I said stupidly—and then swayed on my feet when a neat portal appeared in the air before us. It was maybe four feet tall.

"Very funny, fur-ball," Rans said through gritted teeth. He bent nearly double, forcing me to crouch down to match him. "Mind your head, luv."

We stepped through awkwardly, only to find ourselves standing in the military encampment on the Dhuinne side of the gate. The cat trotted up to the guards watching over the entrance leading back to Earth and meowed, sounding for all the world like a pet asking to be let outside.

The guy who looked to be in charge of things glared darkly at Rans, making me wonder what had gone down between them when he first arrived. Beyond the phalanx of unfriendly faces, the gateway flared into life. Darkness lay beyond it, but it was the darkness of Earth—the interior of the mound on the Hill of Tara. A place I'd never thought to see again.

"One day, there will come a final reckoning, bloodsucker," the lead guard said in a flat voice.

"Something else to look forward to," Rans muttered, leading me through the reluctant gap that formed as the guards made way for us.

But... wait. This was wrong. I'd come here for one reason and one reason only. The gateway was only a handful of steps away when I set my feet, digging in and halting our forward progress.

"My father—" I began.

Rans rounded on me, his expression furious.

"Your *father*. And did dear old Dad welcome you with open arms, Zorah?" he demanded. "No, of course he bloody didn't! Because if he's here in Dhuinne and he's still alive, then it means he's either been collaborating, or he's already broken!"

My throat closed up at the memory of Dad's eyes falling on me.

Why are you here? I don't want you here. Go away.

An injured noise escaped my throat, and I let myself be dragged forward the final few steps and into the gateway. Stepping through it was just as nauseating as I remembered, and when I stumbled out the other side, any benefit I might have been enjoying from vampire blood and Fae magic seemed to have fled.

I leaned over, resting my hands on my knees while my stomach tried to decide whether or not to expel the single mouthful of blood I'd swallowed. Behind me, the light from the gateway faded, and I knew that if I looked, I would once more see an ancient wall etched with Celtic symbols.

"Are we safe now?" I asked, swallowing hard to keep my meager stomach contents in place. "Are there Fae guarding this side of the gate, too?"

"Of course there bloody are," Rans said, pulling me upright and half-leading, half-supporting me along the length of the subterranean gallery. "And I expect we're about as safe here as we were back there."

A meow came from ahead of us, and I realized that the strange cat was still escorting us. I blinked rapidly as we exited the mound, even the cloudy Irish sky seeming too bright after the darkness inside the old burial mound.

We weren't completely alone in the area—what looked like a tour group was gathered next to a collection of standing stones some distance away, listening raptly to the guide as she spoke. A few people at the back of the crowd noticed us, pointing in our direction and leaning their heads together to speak.

The cat, I realized. *They're looking at the cat.*

Were the tourists actually glamoured Fae? Or the tour guide? I huddled more closely against

Rans' side and tried to focus on putting one leaden foot in front of the other. We walked past a church surrounded by a copse of trees. Just beyond it lay a collection of shops with a small parking lot nestled between the buildings.

Rans led me to a nondescript silver sedan and opened the driver's side door, easing me down into the seat. I was confused for a moment about why the hell he thought I was in any condition to drive, but there was no steering wheel on this side. Right. *Ireland.* The cars were backwards here, like in the UK.

I hunched sideways in the seat, trying to gather my strength to lift my heavy legs and swing them inside. The cat twined around my ankles, its chest rumbling with a low purr.

Rans shooed it away. "Yes, yes. You got us here safely. Thanks *ever* so much. Now do me one last favor and sod off, all right?"

The creature rumbled a little growl and trotted off, the tip of its tail twitching. It was true that the cat hadn't made me itch with discomfort the way the Unseelie Fae did, but I still couldn't help relaxing as the last tangible reminder of Dhuinne and its inhabitants disappeared from view around a corner.

Rans reached down and lifted my legs into the car, closing the door without a word. He went around to the other side and reached into the back seat, coming up with a plastic shopping bag. After sliding into the right-hand driver's seat, he set the bag between us, and retrieved car keys from behind the sun visor.

"Did you eat or drink anything they gave you?" he asked, snapping off the words.

"No," I rasped.

"Good." He pulled out a plastic bottle of sports drink, a banana, and a bag of greasy potato chips. "Drink that. Eat this. And don't fucking talk to me right now, because I'm pissed off enough that I might accidentally put the car in a ditch if you do."

Sixteen

I swallowed against the painful dryness of my throat and took the food and drink. My hands were shaking with reaction and weakness, but my desperate thirst—and maybe my horror at the idea of having to ask Rans for help after that last declaration—lent me the strength to twist the cap off the fluorescent blue sports drink.

I tried to sip slowly, not wanting to turn my queasy stomach the rest of the way against me, but instinct took over when the lukewarm liquid hit my tongue. Before I knew it, I was gulping it down, little rivulets escaping to dribble over my chin and drip on my lap. I fell on the food next, shoving it into my mouth, salty and sweet and not nearly enough to fill the gaping hole left by days of starvation.

When it was gone, I put the detritus back in the bag and set it in the foot well. Then, I wrapped my arms around myself, hugging tight. My eyes slid to Rans' profile and away. Eventually, I let my head rest against the window's cool glass, green hills and trees sliding past my unfocused eyes. My stomach churned, and my mind shied away from all the things I should be thinking about right now.

I drifted in that uncomfortable state as we drove through Ireland's rolling rural landscape, thousands of miles away from the place I'd always called home and never expected to see again. Eventually, the car pulled onto a single-lane dirt road, and from there, onto something that could better be described as a track.

I slumped boneless in the seat, letting the ruts and potholes jostle me until Rans brought us to a halt in front of a rustic cottage. I stared at the building stupidly, making no move to open the car door and get out as I took in the acres and acres of nothingness surrounding it. Well… almost nothingness. I could see some white blobs in the distance, like little cotton balls. I think they might've been sheep.

Rans' door opened and closed. He came around to open mine before looking down at me with an unreadable expression. "Do I need to carry you?"

I scowled. "I can walk, goddamn it."

He gave a minute shrug and turned on his heel, heading for the front door of the little house. I watched him retrieve a key from above the lintel and disappear inside.

And now I had to make good on my little moment of defiance.

Fuck.

My entire body felt like it had rusted into immobility during the journey here. How was it that I could have been doing yoga and self-defense training mere days ago, only to feel like this now? Even after drinking and eating, I was still a complete wreck. For the first time, it occurred to me to wonder how much of my weakness was due to starvation and dehydration, and how much was due to the magic Caspian's goon had used on me. Had they managed to damage me permanently somehow, after all?

A chill of fresh fear washed over me. What had the Fae done to me in their eagerness to find out what they wanted to know? Would I recover on my own, or would I just... always feel like this from now on?

Hatred for the blond-haired bastard who'd hurt me followed close on the heels of fear, and it was hatred that gave me the strength to climb out of the car. I tried to slam the sedan's door, but it didn't close all the way. I left it as it was, ignoring the way the little gap between the door and the car's frame mocked me.

Rans had left the front door of the cottage open, but he hadn't returned to check on me despite the fact that it was taking me a ridiculously long time to move.

Good, I thought viciously. I didn't want him to come back. I was angry and confused and exhausted and in pain. I wanted to crawl into a fucking hole and never crawl back out.

I'd made a decision... taken *action* for once in my pathetic life, and done something to try and protect the people I cared about. What a shock that it had backfired on me, and might well have left those people in even more danger than before, right? And here I was, stubbornly *not dead* like I was supposed to be, which meant I was going to have to deal with the fallout of my actions.

But I couldn't face any of it right now. Hell, I could barely *stand up* right now, and I'd chased away the only shoulder that was available for me to lean on. I eyed the short cobblestone walkway leading to the front door, and the grass on either side of it. It was a testament to the state I was in that I seriously considered lying down on that grass and saying *fuck it* to the world for a few hours.

But, no.

I eyed the distance between the car and the nearest wall, and pushed off. My knees wavered, but I aimed the resulting stagger in the direction I needed to go, and the wall hit me before the ground did. The wood-plank siding was rough against my palms, reminding me unpleasantly of the tree-cell. By the time I made it to the open door, I had no doubt that I'd acquired a bunch of new splinters to add to my collection. But I was fucking well going to walk through that door under my own steam if it killed me.

I made it inside, but any delusions I'd had of entering to an impressed audience of one vampire were dashed as I gripped the doorframe and looked around at the place. It was tiny—even smaller than the Fae cottage where Dad was being kept.

I clenched my jaw at the unwelcome reminder of one of the many ways I'd failed, and pushed the thought away. In front of me lay a cozy room with a living area with a large hearth on one side, a cooking area with a second exterior door on the other, and a small table with two chairs set in between.

Three interior doors were set in the far wall. Through the left one I could see the end of a bed.

Through the center one was a bathroom. The rightmost one was firmly and pointedly shut. Even in my current state, I could read the message contained in those tea leaves *just fine,* thanks.

I kicked the front door closed with a clumsy movement of my foot, and used the conveniently placed table as a resting spot in my final push to get from the front door to the empty bedroom. When I made it, I closed the bedroom door behind me with more force than was strictly necessary, because *fuck it all.* Fuck this. Fuck Rans. Fuck *the world.*

Fuck me.

My eyes fell on an overnight bag. The very same bag I'd abandoned in Chicago when I left with Albigard for Dhuinne. The bag Rans had apparently dragged halfway around the world to a bolt-hole in rural Ireland. My eyes burned, the room growing blurry around me.

No. Fuck all of it.

I stumbled to the bed and fell facedown onto it, fully clothed and probably stinking to high heaven after days of imprisonment and terror. There was no way I'd be able to sleep right now, I thought. Not with so many terrible things swirling around the edges of my mind like ravenous carrion birds sensing a meal.

Darkness swallowed me almost before I'd completed the thought.

When I awoke, it was dark. I had no idea what time it was now, or what time of day it had been when we arrived—only that it had been daylight. I was hungry and thirsty, and it felt as though a small, furry animal had crawled into my mouth and died of some horrific disease.

With tentative movements, I rolled over and sat up. The terrifying weakness had eased a bit, to the point that I now felt more like I was recovering from a nasty bout of flu, as opposed to being at death's door. My stomach growled when I registered the smell of something rich and delicious wafting under the closed door.

Was that what had woken me?

The cramping hunger pangs in my belly drove me to shaky feet, propelling me with single-minded purpose toward the source of that mouth-watering aroma. I didn't even stop to think that venturing out of my bedroom would probably mean interacting with Rans until I entered the main room to find it empty.

My eyes shot to the third door; the one that had been closed before. It was open, and also empty. Rans wasn't here.

That might have worried me more if it weren't for the pot warming on the stove. A single light over the counter area illuminated my surroundings—clearly, this place at least had electricity and running water, for all its isolation and rustic charm.

I lifted the lid from the pot, revealing soup. It looked and smelled like vegetable beef, hints of marjoram and thyme teasing my nose. It wasn't as though it could have been meant for anyone else, so I rummaged around in the cabinets and found a bowl, a spoon, and a wooden ladle that had seen better days.

The small fridge held an assortment of bottled water along with more sports drinks. I grabbed some water and carried my small feast to the table. The light above the counter barely reached the dining area, but the dimness suited my mood right now.

I ate and drank, going back for seconds and eventually thirds. I felt like one big, gaping hole that needed to be filled up before I could focus on anything else. And—oh yes—I was painfully, *viscerally* aware of how many things required my focus right now. But at the moment, the soup was here, while the person who could answer at least some of the many questions I had was not.

I finished the entire damned pot of soup, along with two bottles of water. When I was done, I dutifully washed the pot, bowl, and utensils, setting them to dry in one side of the sink. Then I succumbed to paranoia and peeked out a front window just to confirm that the car was still there.

It was.

My eyes scanned the darkness outside, illuminated only faintly by the moon as it played tag with banks of clouds. There was no sign of glowing blue eyes… no silhouette of a brooding figure in my field of view. I could have made a circuit of the other windows in the house to check—or just gone outside and walked around the cottage—but Rans had made it clear enough he wanted space.

Besides, now that my stomach no longer felt like a black hole, exhaustion was hitting me again. The soft bed I'd collapsed in earlier suddenly sounded a whole lot more appealing than playing hide and seek in the dark with a pissed-off vampire. I left the kitchen light burning and headed back to my room, pausing this time to undress and pull on an oversized t-shirt before climbing under the covers.

Jesus. I desperately needed a shower. Unfortunately, the moment I touched the bed, my body seemed to grow heavier and heavier until my arms and legs were too difficult to lift. My eyes slid closed once more.

Daylight. Once again, the smell of food reached my nostrils. Oatmeal, maybe? My stomach rumbled, and I began to wonder how much food it would take to convince my body that it wasn't being starved anymore.

I felt a little stronger than I had when I got up during the night. As tempting as the smell of breakfast was, the smell coming from my armpits really needed to be dealt with first. I poked my head out of the room, but the little cottage still had that quiet feeling of emptiness about it. The door to Rans' bedroom was once more standing open. The main room was devoid of life.

I went into the bathroom to scope out the bathing options. An old claw-foot bath had been outfitted with a shower nozzle on a freestanding metal arm, positioned so it would rain down over the center of the tub. There was no shower curtain to prevent splashes, but the tiled floor sloped down to a drain in the center of the small room.

Good enough for me.

The water pressure sucked, but it was at least nice and hot. Scrubbing at the days of grime, I let it flow over my head and face, blocking out the rest of the world. The soap and shampoo options were basic, but I had some leave-in conditioner in my luggage. Brittle hair probably shouldn't be my biggest worry now, regardless.

I dried off and wrapped the towel around myself before returning to my room. Not gonna lie, here—the silence of this place was starting to get to me. I took comfort in the familiar ritual of moisturizing and picking out my curls, then I noticed something folded up in the corner of my bag.

It was Rans' shirt—the one I'd stolen as revenge after he tore my nightgown. Chewing my lip, I debated for several moments before pulling it out. It smelled like him, with a faint hint of my body lotion layered over his scent from when I'd worn it briefly back in Chicago. I put it on and buttoned all but the top two buttons.

The pot was back on the stove. As I'd suspected, it contained oatmeal. Since my dietary choices still seemed to be relatively low on the list of things likely to kill me, I ladled up a bowl and grabbed a sports drink from the fridge, wishing briefly for orange juice instead.

After blowing on the first spoonful of oatmeal and popping it in my mouth, I made a face and reached for the cheerful little sugar bowl sitting in the center of the table with the salt and pepper. Rans had salted the oatmeal but not sweetened it at all. I wondered if that was an Irish thing... or maybe a Middle Ages thing. With the addition of what was probably too much sugar to counteract the salt, it was surprisingly good.

So... now I was fed, rested, and bathed. Which meant I was quickly running out of excuses and distractions. Real life was going to come crashing back down on my head before long, I was certain.

I staved it off for a few more minutes by brushing and flossing my teeth. Then I repeated the faintly ridiculous ritual of checking that the car hadn't moved, because seriously—did I think the oatmeal had cooked itself? It was still parked in the same place.

The morning was beautiful. So was the landscape around the cottage. Yesterday's gray clouds had given way to brilliant sunshine, turning the blue of the sky and the green of the fields to jewel tones.

For the lack of anything better to do, I pulled on some shorts under the oversized button-down shirt and padded outside barefoot. It was pleasantly cool here. Much cooler than it would have been in St. Louis or Chicago in late June.

That gave me pause. It was the end of June, though I couldn't honestly have said what the exact date was. But I knew it was almost July. It was almost the twentieth anniversary of my mother's death. A thick feeling clogged my throat, and I swallowed hard to clear it.

I couldn't face all the things that came along with that realization just now, so I started walking instead of thinking.

It wasn't obvious whether this place was a farmhouse attached to the surrounding lands, or just someone's private getaway retreat. There were indeed sheep wandering in some of the fields in the distance, but I didn't see any outbuildings nearby for keeping animals or equipment. That probably meant it wasn't a farm.

The area around the cottage was landscaped, with stone paths and hedges and a few carefully placed shade trees. Flowers dotted the meticulously maintained beds at the bases of the trees. My mind flickered back to the choking plant life of Dhuinne, and I shook my head sharply to dislodge the image.

Someone—okay, *Rans,* since no one else was here—had closed the passenger-side door of the car properly, after I'd left it unlatched. I wandered around the side of the cottage, noting that the kitchen door led onto a little stoop. Beyond lay a modest herb garden. The smell of lavender and basil wafted through the air, carried on the light breeze.

The land behind the house was just grass. No effort had been made here with landscaping, although there was a weathered wood-and-wrought-iron bench set facing toward the rolling green hills beyond.

A figure sat halfway up the nearest hill, picked out in black and white. *Rans.*

I swallowed hard and walked toward him, the soft grass tickling my bare toes. He was dressed similarly to the first time I'd ever seen him, minus the gruesome bloodstains—dark jeans, white shirt, black leather vest, combat boots. His knees were drawn up, forearms resting on them limply as he gazed out across the valley. He didn't look at me as I approached—not even when I sat down next to him, separated by an arm's length, my joints creaking in protest.

"So," I said, when the silence grew too stifling. "Are we still doing the not-talking-about-it thing?"

He was quiet for a long moment. Then he finally glanced over at me, and his gaze dropped from my face to the shirt I was wearing. After a beat, he looked away again, staring into the distance instead.

"Still experiencing incandescent rage whenever I try to think about the last three days," he said eventually, "so continued silence on the subject would probably be the best plan, yes."

I pondered that for a minute. "Okay," I said, not sure how else to really answer.

The silence stretched again, even longer than before.

"It reminds me of home a bit, this place," he said at length.

I didn't know what to say to that, either.

We sat, separated by three feet and the unspoken gulf of my betrayal. When it became obvious that neither of us had anything else to contribute to the conversation, I climbed inelegantly to my feet and walked back down the hill to the cottage.

Once inside, I nosed around the place, poking into closets and drawers. I was getting more and more of a 'vacation home' vibe from the little house, with the way it was furnished just enough for someone to be able to stay here comfortably, without so much as a hint of anything personal.

There was also precious little in the way of entertainment to be had. No TV, no radio, no computer, no bookshelves. Who normally stayed here, I wondered? I could maybe picture it as a writer's retreat—a place with distractions so few and far between that someone might pound out an entire novel through sheer desperation to keep the boredom at bay.

That made me think about the copy of *Sherlock Holmes* I'd bought in Atlantic City. Was it still in my bag?

To my relief, it was. I grabbed a bottle of water and retreated to the worn couch in the living area, angling myself so sunlight from the open window fell across the yellowed pages. I read for a couple of hours, only stopping when I felt the burn of angry tears as I read about Charles Augustus Milverton's downfall and found myself picturing Caspian in the villain's place.

I set the book aside listlessly, staring instead at the pattern of bumps on the plaster ceiling until it all started to blur together. I must have fallen into a doze, because I woke to find the sun no longer illuminating the room through the east-facing window. Rans was seated in the chair set at right angles to the couch, watching me over steepled fingers.

I blinked several times in rapid succession and straightened self-consciously from my casual sprawl, feeling my muscles and joints howl in protest. Blue eyes tracked the movement, but I couldn't read the expression behind them.

"This is stupid," I said, my voice raspy. "And you're being a bit of a creeper right now with the whole *watching me sleep while you're angry at me* thing. I got enough of that kind of creepy shit from the faeries."

His face darkened, and *that* expression was easy enough to read. *Fury*. Ah, well. We might as well have it out now rather than later, I supposed.

"Tell me what you did back there with the crystal," I ordered, before he could open his mouth and remind me again how pissed off he was at me. "What the hell is a life-bond?"

His hands fell to rest on his knees, and those icy eyes narrowed. "It's the thing that's keeping your head attached to your shoulders. Now—your turn. Tell me why you went behind my back in an attempt to commit suicide. Or maybe *suttee* would be a better term?"

I frowned at him. "I don't know what that means."

He raised an eyebrow. "*Suttee*—the outdated Hindu practice of immolating oneself on a loved one's funeral pyre as some ill-conceived act of solidarity." The words were bitten off in that precise English accent, sharp as knives.

"That's not what I was doing," I said.

"Wasn't it?" he asked.

Now *I* was angry. "No! Why the hell would you think that?"

The furrow between his brows deepened. "Why would I think that? Possibly because you disappeared while I was sleeping in order to go to a place where you knew your life would be in immediate and mortal danger, in pursuit of someone who is most likely incapable of giving a tinker's damn about you or your wellbeing."

I surged to my feet, ignoring the sharp pains in my knees and hips at the sudden movement.

"Fuck you, Rans!" I snarled. "I left to try and keep you safe—not just to find out what happened to Dad!"

He was on his feet and in my face so fast I barely registered the movement. "To keep *me* safe... can you even hear yourself?"

His voice was a cold growl as he loomed over me, using his height to advantage.

I shoved at his chest, suddenly enraged. Of course, I grew even more enraged when my shove failed to move him an inch. Instead, I was the one who stumbled back half a step.

"And how did that grand gesture work out for you?" he continued relentlessly.

I shoved at him again, with exactly the same result.

"I had it under control!" I practically yelled. "Albigard was going to try to get Dad out for me, and you were supposed to stay away!"

His eyes flared with inner light at the mention of Albigard's name, and he caught my wrist when I pulled my fist back to punch him in the chest.

His tone was low and rough when he said, "I did *not* rescue you from Caspian in St. Louis just so you could seduce one of my few allies into betraying me, Zorah."

Guilt and fury warred in my stomach. I hauled off and slapped him as hard as I could with my free hand. An instant later, I grunted as my back impacted the front door with a thump. Rans had swung me around in the blink of an eye and now held me pinned against the worn wood, my wrists held in an unbreakable grip above my head, our bodies pressed together from chest to knee.

"Fucker," I whispered, right before his mouth crashed into mine.

Seventeen

I growled and kissed him back, feeling the sudden uncontrollable desire to… just… burn everything between us to the ground. His body was hard against mine. Unforgiving. I bit his lip with enough force to draw blood, and his dick twitched against my stomach. He wrenched away, pulling me with him, whirling me around to face away from him and pushing me against the back of the couch.

I gasped, my body folding in half at the hips over the back of the sofa—ass in the air, upper body splayed over the cushions so that my hair brushed against the worn fabric. I braced my hands on the seat cushions as fingers grasped the waist-band of my loose shorts and yanked them down. The sound of a zipper behind me followed.

Jesus Christ. I was wet… *so wet.* I keened when Rans' hard cock slammed into me, clawing at the upholstery beneath my fingers as the gaping pit of my need opened up and threatened to swallow us both whole.

I cursed and cried out at the brutal thrusts pounding into me, wanting to reach out with my succubus nature and rip Rans' desire out of his body by the roots so I could drag it into mine. I wanted to draw and draw on it, until the pit of emptiness inside me was full of something besides my own fear and failure. His hands gripped my hips with bruising strength, holding me in place as my bare toes scrabbled against the slick hardwood floor.

It was hard to breathe… but I didn't need to breathe. I just needed him to keep fucking me like this. When his movements slowed, then stopped, I groaned in protest, writhing against him as his upper body leaned forward to drape over mine. He was trembling faintly.

"Damn you, Zorah Bright." The words were a low rumble against the back of my neck.

But if I was part demon, it meant I was already damned, didn't it?

One of his arms wrapped around my chest. He used that grip around me as leverage to pull my upper body nearly upright while his lower body continued to pin my hips in place against the back of the couch. The angle of his cock inside me shifted, drawing a hard shudder from me.

He drew my arms backward, looping a forearm through the crook of my left elbow and across my back to grasp my right bicep in an unbreakable hold. My breasts jutted out as the position forced my shoulders back, but I forgot all about the strain when he rolled his hips, thrusting deep. The movement punched a breathless sound from my throat.

I'd wanted something to fight against. I'd *needed* it. So I struggled and panted against the hold restraining me, and the cock filling me up. The hand that had been wrapped around my chest grabbed one edge of the stolen shirt I was wearing and jerked. Buttons popped, some hitting the couch cushions, others falling to the wood floor with a scattering of tiny noises as they bounced and skittered in every direction.

A cool palm—rough with calluses—ran possessively over my breasts and stomach, claiming my body even as I squirmed and writhed. A hard shaft rocked into me, pressing my pelvis against the lightly padded frame of the sofa back. I could feel my body drawing on his—taking... taking... making me feel drunk with the heady mixture of anger, lust, and pain swirling between us.

Rans continued to run his free hand over my body, squeezing and kneading my tits, then sliding up to encircle my throat—daring me not to trust him with this. I swallowed, my head falling back, feeling the movement push against the cool weight of his palm. My pulse throbbed beneath the light pressure of his fingers and thumb.

Using the grip he had on my arms, he pulled my back flush against his front. Now every sharp thrust of his cock rolled my clit against the back of the couch, which was starting to scoot against the floor with a series of harsh squeaks.

I was floating, falling, dizzy with the need to tear both of us down until nothing was left. Rans' cock pounded against my G-spot, combining with the pressure against my clit to drive me inexorably toward something ugly and devastating... and painfully, inescapably necessary. I could feel him rushing toward the same cliff, desperate and self-destructive.

He groaned—an animal noise. His hand around my throat dragged my head to the left. An instant later, his fangs sank into the juncture of my neck and shoulder with the unexpected abruptness of a striking snake.

I shrieked and struggled and came; fought and sobbed and came even harder, my pussy clamping around his dick while his jaws clamped around my flesh. Every muscle in my body went taught as I felt him follow me into release, pouring his animus into me as he growled against my bitten flesh.

We ended up in a sweaty heap, still draped over the back of the couch. Tears traced rivulets down my face, while two dribbles of blood trailed down my right breast from the twin punctures in my shoulder.

"I'm afraid I'll get you killed if you stay," I rasped eventually, my voice completely wrecked.

Rans rested his forehead against my back for a long moment. I felt cool breath sigh out against my skin, chasing shivers down my spine.

"Yes… well. It does seem rather unavoidable now," he said. "Though it hardly matters if I stay or leave at this point."

And then he was lifting me upright, steadying me on my feet, still holding me facing away from him, his arms wrapped around me from behind. I stood there, very still, with bruises on my hips, blood on my chest and my sex aching from the abuse it had just received. How fucked up was it that I now felt about a hundred times better than I had before?

It was really, really fucked up, I decided. But that didn't make it any less true. Fresh strength flooded my limbs, the pain and creakiness in my joints a fast-fading memory. My mind felt clearer, my head no longer ached, and the insatiable pit lurking in my chest and belly no longer threatened to consume me from the inside out.

"Please talk to me properly now," I whispered.

I felt the softening of his stance at my back—felt him giving in.

"I will, Zorah," he promised quietly.

The shower in the little cottage might have been fairly lackluster, but the water coming from the tap was hot, and the old claw-foot tub was big enough for two. I lay back between Rans' legs, resting against his chest and letting the water lap against my chin. With luck, the warm bathwater would help to soak away the chill of what I suspected I was about to learn.

Rans' voice was low and even. "A life-bond is an unbreakable connection between two individuals. It's forged through the exchange of blood, and sealed using a certain kind of crystal imbued with demon magic. It becomes permanent upon the destruction of that crystal."

I swallowed. "So… when you talked about my death causing your death, you were being literal?"

"Very." His hands didn't move from where they rested across my belly.

"Where did you get the crystal?" I asked, as a way to avoid the question that I really needed answered.

"I stole it. From Nigellus. I stopped in Atlantic City on my way from Chicago to Dublin." He paused for a beat. "Of course, I expect he'll be quite cross once he notices it's missing. Especially since I had the unmitigated cheek to ask for the use of this cottage right after I'd nicked it."

Great. So I'd managed to drive a wedge not only between Rans and Albigard, but him and Nigellus as well.

I steeled myself. "I'm human, Rans. Well, mostly. Even if I don't get killed before then, I'll die of old age in fifty or sixty years. If we're... magically tied together somehow, what happens to you then?"

His voice was level. "About what you'd expect."

Denial suffused me, and I twisted in his grip. "*Why would you do that?*"

He met my gaze and held it. "Why would you sneak away behind my back and go to Dhuinne?"

I pushed away from his body, scooting around to sit at the other end of the tub, facing him—our legs tangled together under the water. Unfortunately, if I'd wanted space, a bathtub had probably been an unwise venue for the discussion, but *oh, well.*

"I told you," I said. "I needed to find Dad, and I wanted to make sure you wouldn't get killed trying to protect me when and if Caspian and his goons found us and descended in force."

So instead, he's going to get killed whenever I end up getting killed... whether that's tomorrow or decades from now. Good one, Zorah.

My throat grew tight.

"You should have talked to me instead of running," he said in a low tone. Then he sighed, and eased back, consciously relaxing his frame. "How did you manage it, anyway? You didn't take money, or even Guthrie's credit card."

There was no point in trying to hide the details from him. Not now.

"When you gave me your phone after we left the newspaper office in Chicago and sent me ahead to the car, I thought it would be a good idea to transfer some of the important phone numbers to my burner phones for emergencies," I explained. "You told me to call A.C. if you didn't come back. That was obviously Nigellus. Guthrie was in there, too, and it wasn't hard to figure out who Tink was supposed to be."

"Ah."

"It was pretty obvious that Nigellus and the other people you talked to that night weren't going to be able to help us. Not without taking forever, anyway. You knew it. I knew it," I continued. "My dad had already been in Fae custody for days. I went outside and called Albigard while you were asleep. It was sheer luck that he actually picked up his phone. I asked him if he could get me into Dhuinne and try to arrange some kind of exchange—me for my father. He said he'd try."

"I will rip the points off his fucking Fae ears and pin them to his skull with rusty iron nails." Rans' voice was still even and low.

I narrowed my eyes. "*Why*? Why blame him for doing exactly what I asked him to?"

His blue gaze was hard. "Because it was mercenary and self-serving of him. If you think he was doing it as some kind of favor, you've got a lot to learn about the Fae."

"I didn't ask him for a favor! I asked him if he thought he could do it, and he said it was possible. It wasn't like he was trying to lure me into going with him!" I insisted.

I wondered if being a vampire meant you didn't have to blink, just like you didn't have to breathe—because it was becoming awfully hard to hold those glacier-deep eyes with mine.

It became even harder when he said, "I woke up to find you gone, but all your belongings had been left behind. There was no sign of a struggle. Still, I could only conclude that the Fae had managed to sneak in and take you, while I lay insensate mere meters away, drooling on my pillow like some kind of lack-wit after I'd vowed to myself that I'd protect you."

Guilt tugged at me with more insistence. "Well… a Fae *did* sneak in and take me, but only because I asked him to." My gaze slid away from his, despite my best efforts. "I should have left you a note, or something. I'm sorry. I'd expected to have to sneak back inside the house to get money for a cab. But Albigard just… showed up, the moment I ended the call. Portaled right into the back yard, because I guess the mead I accepted from him means he can find me anytime he likes, now."

"Yes," Rans agreed. "It does."

I swallowed. "Anyway, it happened so fast that I just went with him. I didn't want to have time to start second-guessing myself because, not to put too fine a point on it, I was scared shitless by that point."

He was silent for a few moments.

"Fear is there to keep you from doing stupid things," he said eventually. "You should have listened to that fear instead of ignoring it."

But I shook my head. "Maybe that's true for normal people. People who aren't messed up, I mean. But when you've spent a lifetime being afraid, you either learn to move past it, or you never accomplish a goddamned thing. You wither away until only the fear is left."

He didn't reply, so I continued.

"Why did you come after me, Rans? I told you why I did what I did, but why did you do what *you* did? You accused me of trying to commit suicide, but you've just sentenced yourself to death within the next few decades by tying your life to mine."

I was still having trouble holding his gaze, but I caught the way his eyebrow arched.

"You're not worried that I might have sentenced *you* to death instead? It goes both ways, Zorah. If I die, so do you."

I waved the words away, though. "You've made it seven hundred years, Rans. Black Death and shotgun blasts and all. Seems like most of the risk here is on your end."

"It was a calculated risk."

I wasn't so ready to let it go. "Oh, yeah? About that… I might've been pretty far out of it, but it wasn't lost on me that you didn't know for sure about your survival being a treaty provision. What was it you said to the Magistrate? '*I thought it must be something like that*'?"

He shrugged, though I noticed that it was his turn to glance away.

"There are only so many reasons why the winning army in a supernatural war would leave one single member of an enemy race alive when they clearly have the means to snuff him out at any time."

I digested that for a moment. "The winning army? I thought Nigellus called the war a *messy draw*."

The bark of laughter Rans let out had nothing to do with amusement, I could tell.

"You've seen enough to form your own opinions about that, I'd imagine," he said. "Fae are taking over your world, Zorah. More and more each year."

"It's your world, too," I whispered. But he was right, of course. Admittedly, Nigellus was the only demon I knew, but he was holed up in a vice-ridden enclave with his aging butler, staying out of everyone's way. And for all his obvious wealth and charisma, he hadn't even been able to help us with getting Dad back. All of which was just a distraction from what was truly important in this conversation.

"So, you charged into the Fae Court and bound your life to a mortal's because you thought that *maybe* there was a reason they hadn't killed you yet, beyond luck or laziness," I said. "I get that you're angry with me. You have every right to be. But I'm allowed to be angry with you, too. You did the same freaking thing to me that I did to you—putting your life at risk to try and protect mine. And I still don't understand *why*!"

The look he gave me was almost pitying.

"Bloody hell, Zorah. Why do you *think*?" he asked.

And with that, he had me—because I didn't dare say aloud the thing I was thinking. It was stupid and naive, and if I were wrong... if he laughed in my face, it would be way, *way* too painful.

"I'm starting to feel kind of tired again," I muttered... coward that I was.

He sighed, his chest rising and falling under the water for reasons that had nothing to do with the need for oxygen. "Go eat something and then come to bed. You're still recovering."

"What? You're not going to cook for me this time?" I asked, striving for a lighter mood.

He tried on a smile, though it couldn't quite hide the dark nature of his thoughts. "I'm afraid that between reheating tinned soup and cooking instant porridge, you've plumbed the depths of my culinary expertise. To say that I'm a bit rusty in the kitchen these days is an understatement."

We were both trying too hard, but I guess that was better than giving each other the silent treatment... or breaking random furniture in the cottage with angry sex. I got out of the tub and made a point of stealing the shirt Rans had been wearing earlier to replace the one that was now missing two-thirds of its buttons.

He watched me with heavy-lidded eyes from his careless sprawl in the tub. "Vixen," he accused, though his voice sounded tired.

"What?" I asked, wrapping a towel around my hair so it wouldn't drip. "The other shirt is yours, too. Even if you're not a whizz in the kitchen, you must've learned how to sew on a button at some point in the last seven hundred years."

With that, I walked out of the bathroom—grateful for any small victory I could come by just now. I was still surrounded by a thousand buzzing worries that threatened to swarm me if I stopped moving long enough to focus on any of them.

What would Rans' reckless actions with the supposedly magic crystal really mean for the two of us, going forward? If someone got to me and decided to kill me despite the nebulous threat to the peace treaty, would he literally just fall over dead? Because I could totally see Caspian saying *fuck it,* and taking matters into his own hands to get rid of me.

And what about my father? Despite my best efforts, I'd been rolling his listless words to me around in my subconscious all day.

Zorah? Why are you here? I don't want you here. Go away.

What had seemed so clear when I was trapped in Dhuinne now seemed much more ambiguous. True, it wasn't a stretch to assume that Darryl

Bright was simply putting a capstone on his two decades of horrible parenting—telling me that he didn't care about me and didn't want to have to see or deal with me, even in such extreme circumstances as his captivity in Dhuinne.

Or else, the traitorously hopeful inner six-year-old inside me prodded, *he could have been trying to warn you away from danger. He could have been saying that he knew things were bad, and he didn't want you to get dragged into it with him.*

I shook my head sharply, nearly dislodging the towel wrapped around my head in the process.

Yeah, *right.*

Except for that one shining moment when he'd sent me money in St. Louis, when had Dad ever played the hero? And if Rans was to be believed, he might well have only pretended to help me as a way to lure me to where Caspian and his men were lying in wait at the bus station. Who was I kidding?

I needed to stop thinking about this. I needed to stop thinking about life-bonds and treaties and the things Caspian had done to me during those awful couple of days in Dhuinne. I puttered around the bedroom, sleepwalking through my post-bathing routine. When I wandered out to raid the kitchen cabinets for more food, I couldn't help glancing through the open bathroom door to see Rans still lying in the antique tub, his head thrown back to rest against the rim with his eyes closed, baring the pale column of his throat.

I also needed to stop thinking about Rans dying. That was a biggie.

Tearing my gaze away, I continued to the kitchen and rummaged around until I found some cereal and fruit. Even after everything else, I still got a stupid little thrill at the idea of eating gluten-rich cereal soaked in dairy, so I stood at the counter and downed a bowl of Whole Grain Shreddies with sliced bananas. 'Delicious crispy squares with a yummy, malty taste,' the cheerful blue box informed me.

The *malty* part wasn't entirely inaccurate, but honestly, *delicious* and *yummy* might have been a bit of a stretch. I took the bowl to the table and poured some sugar from the sugar bowl into the mix, in hopes of making the experience match up to my childhood memories of Sugar Pops and Frosted Flakes a little more closely.

In a moment of whimsy, I wondered if you could buy Lucky Charms in Ireland, because that would be pretty funny, actually.

I'd heard Rans moving around while I was in the kitchen, so I figured he'd gone to one of the bedrooms to wait for me. It was telling that we both seemed to assume the aftermath of violent hate-sex and an uncomfortable conversation in a shared bathtub would involve sleeping in the same room.

But he'd told me to 'come to bed,' rather than 'go to bed.' The implication was clear enough, and when I poked my head into the room I'd claimed as mine, it was to find him already there. I'd turned off all the lights except the one over the kitchen counter. It was still relatively early, the long summer evening not quite ready to cede dusk to night.

Summer. July Fourth. Yet another thing I needed to try not to think about.

I slid in next to the shadowed form resting beneath the sheets. When I drew breath to speak, however, a fingertip pressed over my lips to keep them closed.

"Shh," Rans said. "Not tonight. Whatever it is, it can wait until morning."

I let the trapped breath flow out through my nose, and nodded. Deft hands unbuttoned my purloined shirt, baring my skin to feather-light caresses that traveled the same path as the bruisingly possessive touches he'd used earlier. I fell into the promise of distraction eagerly, reaching out to explore his body in return and finding him naked under the bedclothes.

Full dark fell outside as we did our best to avoid thinking about anything except physical pleasure, and by the time I eventually slipped into sleep, I was as warm and sated as I could ever remember being.

Epilogue

When I woke up the following morning, there was a cat perched on the chair across from the bed.

I blinked, rubbed my eyes, and looked again. The cat was still there, its slanted green eyes and silky black coat worryingly familiar. The angle of the sun outside made me think it was still pretty early, in the 'not a good time of day for vampires' sense of being early. I nudged Rans with my elbow anyway, because I was fucking well *not* going to deal with an intelligent Fae cat burglar on my own.

Especially not while I was naked, and presumably reeked like the morning after a hot vampire sex marathon.

"Rans," I hissed.

"Huh?" Rans rolled into a sitting position next to me. His eyes narrowed, and he glared at the four-legged intruder with an expression that said he was less than happy about being poked awake to deal with something like this first thing in the morning. "Oh, for..."

He grabbed a pillow, as if to throw at the sleek animal.

In a flash, the cat morphed into a pretty, rather androgynous humanoid figure sitting cross-legged in the chair. Short black hair framed a pixie-like face lit by forest-green eyes.

"… what the actual hell?" I asked faintly, too shocked to even think of dragging the sheet over my exposed boobs to cover them.

"Leave now," Rans ground out, "before I forget that I usually like cats."

The pixie-like intruder ignored him, focusing on me instead. "Why did you visit the Fae-kept human in Dhuinne, demonkin?"

I stared back, trying to get my brain in gear. "The… Fae-kept…?" Then, it clicked into place. "Wait. You mean my father?"

The pixie leaned forward, nostrils flaring as though to smell me. "Ah, I see. The human is your sire. Your language is still strange to me, and I didn't notice the resemblance between you beneath the stench of demon."

I leaned back, attempting to get out of sniffing range. The effort only caused my shoulder to bump into Rans' chest.

"I'm about to find something harder and with much sharper edges to throw at you than a pillow," Rans warned our nosy visitor.

I put a quelling hand on his chest. "Hang on. What do you know about my dad?" I asked. "Why were you with him inside that house in Dhuinne? And, uh… what *are* you, exactly?"

Yeah, so that last question might not have been the height of diplomacy. But, then again, neither was torturing someone and sentencing her to execution because of who her grandfather was, so I think I was owed a couple of free passes for manners, at the very least.

"Our friendly neighborhood peeping tom is a cat-sidhe," Rans said, still sounding irritated. "A Fae shape-shifter, in other words."

O-*kay*, then.

I still couldn't make a gender determination. Since it appeared we weren't going to be standing on politeness this morning, I decided to ask rather than keep wondering about it. "Sorry, but are you male or female?"

"No," said the cat person.

Cat faerie.

Whatever.

Either way, I supposed that answered that. "Non-binary. Gotcha. So… about my dad?"

The Fae tilted their head. "Your sire was exchanged for my old Mistress' son when they were both infants. I helped care for him when he was brought to Dhuinne, so she would not risk becoming too attached to him before the Tithe."

I was having difficulty untangling that statement, but Rans stiffened beside me.

"Darryl Bright was replaced with a Fae changeling?" he demanded.

The pixie-faced figure shrugged. "That is what I just said, vampire."

Rans was frowning. "But he lived on Earth. He had a family in the human realm."

"Yes, that is so. My Mistress died unexpectedly, not long after the exchange took place." The Fae's delicate features twitched into a matching frown. "The human titheling's mother had some glimmering of the second sight. She knew the Fae infant was not her son, and she started using magic in an attempt to find out what had happened to her real child. I helped arrange for her son's return to Earth, rather than risk a human learning too much about the Fae world. My Mistress' baby was taken away from the woman and exchanged with a different Earth child, instead."

I lifted my hands in a time-out gesture. "Whoa. Back up. Can someone explain this in words of one syllable for the clueless human, please?"

"You are not human, demonkin," said the Fae.

"I was *raised* human," I shot back. "So just treat me like I am one, for purposes of this conversation—all right?"

But the shape-shifter only looked confused. "If you were a human, we would not be having this conversation in the first place."

I closed my eyes and counted silently backwards from ten. "Rans?" I prompted. "A little help here, please?"

Rans still sounded grim. "You've heard the old tales about fairy-folk stealing human babies, yes?"

"Probably," I replied. "I mean, I was never big on the Brothers Grimm, but it rings a vague bell."

"Well, like many legends about the Fae, there's some truth in it," he went on. "As far as I've been able to determine, the practice is part of their strategy to take control of the human realm from within. Caspian was a changeling, for instance."

I tried to twist my brain around that, looking between Rans and the Fae. "You mean the Fae are planting their own babies in human families and somehow grooming them to become... what? State Auditors?"

Rans let out a huff. "Grooming them to become powerful people, certainly. I sincerely doubt that Golden Boy is on the Missouri Department of Revenue's payroll as anything other than a high-paid consultant with connections in all the right places."

I pondered that. "Still. That's kind of horrifying." I returned my attention to the waiflike shape-shifter. "What happens to the human babies, though? What would have happened to my father if my grandmother hadn't managed to get him back?"

The Fae looked troubled.

"Well?" I pressed. "You said something about your... Mistress... not wanting to become attached to him before the, what was it? The *Tithe*?"

Beside me, Rans had gone very still.

The Fae's voice was so soft I had to strain to hear the words. "Yes. The Tithe to Hell."

"What are you saying?" Rans' tone grew dangerous.

The shape-shifter blinked large, green eyes at him. "The Fae are bound by the treaty to deliver to Hell one child of every ten that are born. That was the price for peace. Well... that and your life, vampire."

Rans flinched almost imperceptibly.

"In order to avoid sending our own children to our sworn enemies," the Fae continued, "we exchange many of our babies for human children, and surrender those souls to the demons, instead."

My heart began to pound so hard that I was sure everyone in the room must have been able to hear it. "Oh, my god. Tell me you're joking," I whispered.

Fine, dark brows drew together. "Why in Mab's name would I joke about such a thing, demonkin?"

My eyes flew to Rans. "This can't possibly be what it sounds like... can it?" I demanded, trying not to fall headlong into a pool of assumptions that might be completely wrong. "I mean—Hell's not really fire and brimstone, right? Nigellus even said so. And... he's not evil. He's your friend."

I'd been hoping for some kind of casual dismissal of my concerns; some scoffing reassurance that this 'Tithe' wasn't what I thought it was. Instead, Rans seemed to have disappeared into that dark place I'd glimpsed on only a couple of occasions, when he was swallowed up by the holes in his own past.

The elfin figure in the chair frowned at us, as though unsure what our problem was. "Your sire's mind was broken when he was returned to Dhuinne, demonkin. Since he is of no more use to the Fae in his current condition, the Unseelie Commander who brought you to the Court has been arguing that he should be thrown in with the next Tithe shipment. Isn't this a good thing? The demons are your allies, after all. Your people. Would you not rather have him in their custody than the Fae's?"

I was seriously running close to mental capacity here, but I made a valiant effort to consider the Fae's words objectively.

"Rans?" I asked, my tone wavering. "Is there some way we can get him back from the demons if that happens?"

He seemed to shake himself free of whatever black hole of memory had swallowed him. "It's... it's possible. I don't know. We can speak to Nigellus—"

I swallowed hard. Nigellus. The *other* person whose friendship with Rans I might've destroyed when I ran off to Dhuinne.

But our uninvited guest clearly hadn't picked up on the uncomfortable subtext.

"That would please me, I think," the shapeshifter said, as though genuinely concerned for my father's wellbeing. "However, you must take care. Many factions will be after the only living being who embodies humanity, demonkind, and Fae at the same time."

"What did you just say?" Rans asked sharply.

But the Fae's attention stayed focused on me. "Demonkin, the only reason your sire could possibly have survived marriage to a cambion—much less impregnated one—is because of the Fae magic he absorbed as an infant during his stay in Dhuinne, before he was returned to Earth."

"*Bloody hell.*" The hoarse whisper made me turn back to find that Rans had gone pale as a sheet.

"What?" I demanded. "What's wrong?"

"What's *wrong*?" Rans echoed in disbelief.

"Yes!" I shot back, my temper flaring. "I mean, who cares if Dad picked up Fae magic via osmosis when he was a baby, or whatever the hell happened? The Fae already want to kill me just for being part demon!"

He was still looking at me like I was nuts.

"Zorah, don't you see?" he said. "If this is true, you've just become the single most important person in the entirety of the three realms. This is far bigger than any of us realized before." He rolled out of bed, apparently unbothered by his nakedness, and started rummaging for clothes. "Get dressed—you and I need to get back to the States and talk to Nigellus. There are forces at play here that could start a war big enough to put the last one to shame."

I caught the bundle of clothing he tossed at me and looked from him to the Fae, then back again.

"I'm sorry, but I'm still not getting it," I told him. "Why does this make me any more important than before?"

He paused in the middle of dressing and came over to take my hands in both of his. I blinked up at him.

"The Fae are sending human children to Hell," he said slowly, his eyes burning into mine. "Human children who've been living in Dhuinne, and may have absorbed Fae magic during their stay... *just like your father.*"

I frowned. "And if Fae magic meant that he was able to get my mom pregnant..."

"Then the Fae may well be unknowingly providing their sworn enemies with the means to grow in number and strength until the balance of power is shifted in their favor, throwing everything into chaos again," Rans finished.

"Oh, my god," I breathed.

"Quite," he agreed.

It was too much to take in, on top of everything I was already worrying about.

Stop, I tried to tell myself. *Think about Dad. Stay focused on that. If the Fae intend to send him to Hell, you'll need to talk to Nigellus anyway. Worry about the rest of it afterward.*

"Okay. Give me fifteen minutes for a shower," I said. "Then I'll be ready to go. I've got my own list of questions for Uncle Demon, and this time I'm not letting things go until I get some better answers from him."

End of Book Two

The story continues in *The Last Vampire: Book Three.*

If you enjoyed this book, you might also like R. A. Steffan and Jaelynn Woolf's other vampire series, *Circle of Blood*. Keep reading for an exclusive excerpt from *Book One: Lover's Rebirth.*

Circle of Blood Excerpt

(*From Chapter* 2)

Della held her breath and gripped the meaty forearm that was wrapped around her chest with clawed hands, trying desperately to pull the gunman's arm away. Even if she had managed to rip herself free, though, she knew that the minute she made a move to get away, the man would blow her head off. She simply held on, fingernails digging into the heavy black material of his shirt, feeling the seconds tick by one at a time, like dripping molasses.

With the gunman behind her, she could see the chaos on the street again. At least ten bodies lay in pools of blood. The dark red puddles seemed to shimmer under the streetlights. It was as though a heat haze had descended on the block, making everything waver in her vision. Her eyes flickered around, going in and out of focus, searching for any sign of the police or a SWAT team. Praying for help.

There was no one. She was alone with the dead, and the deadly. The other gunmen were chasing stragglers down the block and shooting bullets into fallen bodies. They blasted out windows of shops, including the one she and her captor were standing in front of, which caused him to yell in anger at his comrade.

"What are you doing, you stupid fuck! Trying to get me killed? Point that damn thing somewhere else!"

Della gasped aloud, despite trying valiantly to remain silent. She could hear a dull whine developing in her mind, an all-pervasive buzzing noise that drowned out any thought of defending herself. Panic was flooding her, followed by shock, preventing her from formulating any sort of coherent thought.

"Now, time to deal with you, pretty kitty," the man said, jerking Della from behind so that her feet slipped out from underneath her. He dragged her backwards towards the building as she scrambled to find her footing.

"Let me go," she pleaded.

"Not until you've fucking paid for that little trick you pulled earlier, whore," he said, spinning her around to face him. His breath was hot and smelly on her face. She gagged and fought to get away from him, desperate for fresh air.

He slammed her down on the ground, and her head hit the pavement with a sharp crack. She sprawled there for a moment, stunned by the blow. Lights popped in front of her eyes and Della lay completely still, forgetting where she was or what was going on around her.

The sound of gunfire above her jerked her back to reality. The man standing over her had shot at a car that had driven by, blowing out the windshield and passenger-side window.

Della clapped her hands around her head and curled into a ball, her ears ringing from the repeated blasts so close to her.

Suddenly the man was back, kneeling over her and yanking her arms away from her body. She fought back furiously, swinging and clawing at every square inch of him she could reach. He used his body weight to pin her legs down and pressed the gun against her cheek.

"Lie still," he commanded.

Della struggled for a moment more, but went limp when he pressed the barrel harder against her face.

She looked up into the face of pure evil, seeing his cold, blank eyes gazing back at her. There was only dark mirth and chilly indifference to be found there. She knew with complete certainty that she was going to die any moment now.

Out of nowhere, a mist descended around the site of carnage, swirling as if caught in a high breeze, even though everything in the night had gone completely still. It wrapped itself around the man crouched over her, flowing across his face. He jerked his head to the side, completely bewildered, and tried to swipe at the fog. His fingers passed straight through it, but the mist blew on towards the middle of the street, drawing his gaze. By the way the other gunmen were staggering around and waving their arms, Della guessed that something similar had happened to them.

The mist seemed to solidify in a dense patch in the middle of the blocked street, coalescing to reveal five dark figures. A strange aura of power radiated from them. Several of the gunmen backed away, raising their weapons.

"What the fuck, Benson?" one yelled in confusion in the direction of Della's attacker.

The man called Benson grabbed Della by the hair and dragged her to her feet. She shrieked in pain, clamping her hands around his and scrambling desperately for purchase, trying to find her feet and support her weight.

"Don't just stand there! Kill them!" Benson roared.

All at once, the shadowy figures burst into motion. Their speed was inhuman, Della realized with a jolt. No one could run that fast, not even if they were being pushed by a huge dump of adrenaline. They were moving *unnaturally* fast, almost as if they were flying towards the cluster of gunmen.

Della watched in open-mouthed awe as two women in the group launched themselves at the man carrying the assault rifle. He stumbled back in shock and fired off several rounds, all of which missed the newcomers and buried themselves in a building across the street with an explosion of brick dust. One of the women used a powerful blow to turn the barrel of the rifle towards the ground and slammed her fist into the man's face. His nose erupted in a gush of blood. He fell back onto the ground and both women landed on top of him.

The man who appeared to be in charge of the group of newcomers surveyed the scene with startling light gray eyes that seemed to glow silver in the low light. He effortlessly swept the legs out from underneath the gunman standing closest to him before his pale gaze fell on Della and her captor. Benson growled and raised his gun, pointing it at the man with a shaking hand.

"Help the woman," the silver-eyed newcomer said, apparently unconcerned by the threat. His tone was deep and rich. Crushed velvet over tempered steel.

Somewhere in the back of Della's overwrought brain, she realized that he had the most amazing voice she had ever heard. She would have probably gone weak at the knees if she weren't already shaking like a leaf in a high wind.

Della heard a rushing sound and blinked. When she opened her eyes, a large man was standing in front of her, looking at her attacker with the intense green eyes of a hunting tiger. He took a calculated step forward, fists clenched as if he were about to strike. Benson stepped backwards, pulling her with him, and Della could feel him trembling against her. He fired off another deafening round from his handgun, and her would-be rescuer jerked to the side as it hit him in the chest, under the clavicle.

To Della's utter surprise, the man did not crumple to the ground. Instead, the wound only seemed to make him angrier. He surged forward, grabbing Benson by the head with both hands. Benson dropped Della, who fell to the ground as her tormenter began to scream and struggle wildly, waving the gun around. She rolled quickly out from between the two and watched, horrified, as the newcomer lifted Benson from the ground by his head and threw him into the nearest wall, face first.

He crumpled to the ground—a discarded rag doll, lying in a heap on the dirty pavement, obviously unconscious. The man with the gunshot wound in his chest walked over and stomped his heel down on Benson's face, assuring that he would not be getting up again.

Ever.

The crunch of his skull smashing made Della's stomach churn. She felt bile rising in her mouth and coughed, trying not to vomit. She crawled backwards on her elbows, using her feet to propel her, trying to get away from the grisly tableau.

The movement seemed to catch her rescuer's attention. He walked forward slowly, his hands raised in a peace gesture, and dropped to one knee next to her.

"Hey, now. Easy, there. Are you all right?" His tone was soothing, and very, very British. Della could still feel the aura of raw power radiating from him, which terrified her just as much as the armed man who had taken her hostage. Yet, she could not help but be captivated by his eyes, which seemed almost to glow in the low light. They were mesmerizing, and she realized that she was staring at him like a fool, silent and slack-jawed.

She shook her head, trying to clear it, and raised a hand to her pounding temple.

"Y-yeah, I think so," she answered in a shaking voice.

He knelt next to her.

"It's okay. Take a moment. You've had quite a scare," he said, his voice calm and collected. Della's eyes strayed to the gaping hole under his collarbone, oozing blood that looked almost black in the low light.

"Ah. Yes. Sorry about the gore," he said, noticing her gaze. "It's really unfortunate, that. Smarts like hell, actually, now that I think about it." He winced, lifting a hand to prod at the wound and craning his neck to try to look at it. "Son of a bitch, that's gonna leave a mark. I do *not* get paid enough to deal with this shit while I'm sober…"

Della's mouth was still hanging open, but she couldn't speak. She looked around wildly, wanting nothing more than to just go home and pretend that none of this had ever happened. She felt a bone-deep weariness underneath her pounding heart, and she was still fighting down nausea that threatened to overcome her willpower.

She could see the other figures walking towards her through the darkening evening, all converging on them.

The gray-eyed leader walked over to her rescuer and looked down at the wound on his chest, a crease of worry forming on his forehead. His hair was dark, falling tousled above a serious brow, sharp cheekbones, and full, sensuous lips.

"Xander, you obviously neglected to duck again," he said in that deep velvet voice. "We've talked about this before, have we not?"

Della felt her heart skip a beat despite her terror.

The man called Xander had a hand clamped over the wound now, trying to stem the bleeding. "That we have. And I believe I made it perfectly clear that we need to keep a flask or two of the good stuff on us when dealing with this kind of crap. If I'm going to get shot through the lung by some redneck shithead with crooked teeth and halitosis, I'd prefer to be considerably more intoxicated than this, beforehand."

Ignoring the litany of complaints, the leader knelt and reached out a hand to steady Xander, who had started to sway.

"Well, fuck," Xander said matter-of-factly, and half-collapsed into his friend's supporting grip. Trying to keep both of them upright, the leader set his hand down hard on the ground for balance. His fingers grazed the skin on Della's wrist—the barest of brushes.

It was like touching a live wire. An electric jolt shot through Della's entire body. She felt as though she had been punched in the stomach. Air was forced through her mouth in a sound of shock that was echoed by the leader's surprised grunt. He jerked his hand away and leapt gracefully to his feet with his injured friend held securely in his grip, staring down at Della on the ground as if he had never seen anything like her.

Their eyes met, and she saw something like dismay flicker behind his silver-gray eyes. His lips parted, as if he wanted to say something to her, but no sound escaped his mouth. They stared at each other for several moments, the wounded man next to him flicking his eyes back and forth between the two. His eyebrows furrowed in confusion.

"Tré?" he asked.

The gray-eyed man did not respond, just continued to stare into Della's face. She thought she saw *recognition* flash behind his eyes.

But that was impossible. How could he recognize her? They had never met before. She would have remembered if they had, she was sure.

"*Tré*," The wounded man said, more insistent this time. "Police approaching. Time to leave. Unless you'd like to try answering their questions while I bleed out in the back of a human ambulance?"

This seemed to startle the leader out of his reverie, and he broke eye contact with Della.

"Oksana," he commanded in a hoarse tone. "Wipe her memory."

"Wait. Wipe my *what*?" Della demanded, jerking into a sitting position. She tried valiantly to scramble away from the female figure descending upon her. "No. *No*! Stay away from me."

"It's all right, sweetheart," the woman said in a soothing voice. "Hey, look at me. Relax. That's it."

Della felt all the tightness in her muscles start to drain away. She shook her head, trying to clear it, but a dreamy veil seemed to fall in front of her eyes, making everything foggy.

"No... wait," she said in a weak voice, feeling everything around her grow dim. Grayness seemed to swirl around the edges of her vision and she tried to shake her head again, feeling it flop back and forth in slow motion.

The glare of the streetlights and the chill of the rough pavement beneath her slipped away, sending her into warm, soft darkness.

Want to read more? The complete, six-book *Circle of Blood* series is available now!

To discover more books by this author, visit
www.rasteffan.com

Made in the USA
Middletown, DE
04 February 2020